MAD
About the Major

By Elizabeth Boyle

ELIZABETH BOYLE

MAD
About the Major

AVONIMPULSE
An Imprint of HarperCollins Publishers

Excerpt from *The Knave of Hearts* copyright © 2016 by Elizabeth Boyle.

MAD ABOUT THE MAJOR. Copyright © 2015 by Elizabeth Boyle. All rights reserved under International and Pan-American Copyright Conventions. By payment of the required fees, you have been granted the nonexclusive, nontransferable right to access and read the text of this e-book on screen. No part of this text may be reproduced, transmitted, decompiled, reverse-engineered, or stored in or introduced into any information storage and retrieval system, in any form or by any means, whether electronic or mechanical, now known or hereafter invented, without the express written permission of Harper-Collins e-books.

EPub Edition JUNE 2015 ISBN: 9780062322890

Print Edition ISBN: 9780062322913

10 9 8 7 6 5 4 3

To Terry
After all these years and all these books,
I am, I must confess, still quite mad about you.
Love, E

MAD
About the Major

Chapter 1

London, 1818

"Egads! Kingsley! Is that you?"

Major Kingsley looked up from where he'd been standing, or rather hiding, on the fringes of the ballroom. All around him, the Duke and Duchess of Setchfield's annual masquerade was in full force.

Considering how scandal ridden the ball always seemed to be year after year, Kingsley had come specifically in hopes of finding some lascivious widow or a stray courtesan who'd dared to come mingle in the rarefied air of Mayfair, then wander off for a bit of sport.

It was, after all, his last night of freedom in so many ways.

But it seemed the Fates weren't inclined toward romance this evening as a short, square-figured little man in a bright gold costume came toddling toward him.

There was only one soul on earth who would dare such an ensemble.

"Augie!" Kingsley replied, pushing off the wall, for while this was not quite how he'd envisioned his evening progressing, he was genuinely happy to see his old boon companion. "Well, I never."

Lord Augustus Charles Hustings, or Augie to his friends, was the sort of fellow who always enlivened an evening— what with his nonsensical views and his misguided banter.

Best of all, Augie would never hound a fellow to get married, which was why Kingsley had been loitering about in the shadows—if only to avoid being recognized by some marriage-minded mother with a passel of daughters.

"When did you get back from the Continent?" Augie asked, thumbs tucked into his gold embroidered waistcoat.

"A fortnight ago," the major admitted.

At this, Augie's eyes widened. "And you couldn't call on an old friend after, what? Three, four years?"

"My mother saw me first," Kingsley sheepishly admitted.

Augie snorted, for it was a situation he could hardly condemn anyone else over. His own mother, Lady Prendwick, was a notable handful. "Demmed inconvenient, that. Had you over a barrel, eh?"

"To say the least," Kingsley told him. "My dear *maman* insisted I be kitted out with 'proper' togs for her house party. Supposed to be riding down there tomorrow. You did get your invitation, didn't you?"

Since that particular house party was known by every man in London as a thinly veiled Marriage Mart, where at least three engagements could be counted upon, Augie coughed and pretended he hadn't heard his friend correctly.

Then to change the subject entirely, he glanced at the

major's costume. "Whatever is that you are wearing? Is that the best your mother could command?" His friend shook his head furiously. "Need to find you a new tailor, my good man."

Kingsley laughed, for it seemed that Augie hadn't changed in the least. He reached up and waggled the black piece of silk covering the upper half of his face. "What, my mask isn't dashing enough for you?"

"Hardly," Augie replied, tucking his nose in the air.

"And who are you supposed to be?" he dared to ask, taking a step back and making an inspection—not that it helped, for he was still at a loss as to what Augie's mishmash of gold raiment was supposed to signify.

"Zeus," his diminutive friend announced with great flourish and a stately bow.

Kingsley nearly doubled over with laughter.

Augie frowned, glancing down at his costume to assure himself nothing was amiss. "My valet claims the choice is divinely ironic."

"Yes, something like that," Kingsley agreed as he took another glance around the room and found himself face to face with yet another friend from his days at Eton.

"Kingsley! Dear God! Thought that was you! Wouldn't have recognized you save for this dog in your company." The Honorable Roscoe Evans laughed and nudged Augie aside.

Augie shook his head with annoyance. He didn't find that sobriquet any more amusing now than when Roscoe had come up with it when they were all twelve. "Thought *you* were in the country after that dustup with Lady Verwood. Or rather Lord Verwood." His tone implied he wished him still well away from Town.

Roscoe waved him off. "Nonsense. Not with the Setchfield ball at hand. Always a fair bit of sport to be found, eh, Augie?" He winked, and then turned to the major. "So you are back, aren't you?"

"As observant as ever, Roscoe," Kingsley said, wishing him—as Augie obviously did—well away. For it wasn't that he didn't like Roscoe; he did, in an offhanded fashion.

But wherever Roscoe went, there was always trouble. And right now Kingsley was dancing on the edge of a sword with his parents—who were first and foremost furious with him for not returning home after Waterloo. That he'd taken it in his head to caper about the Continent was a grave sin in their estimation, and one for which it was now time he atoned.

The last thing he needed was an imbroglio to leave him completely at their mercy.

"And unscathed, I see," Roscoe said, glancing sideways at him. "Thought I heard you got shot in that last brush with Boney."

"A scratch or two, nothing of note," Kingsley told him.

"Good news, that. Means you are in fine form for a bit of a wager."

"A wager?" Suddenly Augie's interest came back to life.

Roscoe leaned in. "Mrs. Spenser is here."

"Mrs. Spenser?" Augie shook his head again. Rather like a wet dog, but Kingsley was too well-mannered to point that out. "You're bamming us, Roscoe. Won't fall for any of your capers." He huffed, tucked up his nose, and crossed his arms over his chest, as if to ward off whatever mischief the man proposed.

"No, indeed it is true," Roscoe shot back, all affronted.

"Apparently the duke and duchess attended her ball last month. In disguise of course."

"Of course," Augie agreed, for apparently *that* was old news.

"Yes, well, Mrs. Spenser is here and I have it on good authority that the fellow who unmasks her before midnight gets to uncover the rest of her, if you know what I mean." He nudged Kingsley as if helping him along.

"Yes, yes, I know what you mean. I've been on the Continent, not in a convent," Kingsley told him.

"And have you heard of the lady? Mrs. Spenser?" Roscoe pressed.

"Yes. I've heard of this nonpareil." Kingsley hadn't been in London a day before the tales of Mrs. Spenser and her beauty (along with her lascivious practices) had reached his ears. Exactly the sort of woman he'd come here searching for—the sort he could lose himself with for a night or so . . . before he must absolutely make his way to his mother's house party.

And all that it entailed. Proposed. Demanded.

Roscoe rocked on his boot heels. "I know which lady she is."

"Stuff and nonsense," Augie shot back. "If you know who she is, why haven't you gone and claimed her for yourself?"

"Was going to do just that, then I saw our good friend here." He nodded at Kingsley. "Home from the war, I said to myself. Served his King and country with heroism—if the newspapers are to be believed. Be rather selfish of me not to offer her up to our own Major Kingsley, a thank-you as it were."

Augie snorted.

Kingsley laughed in skeptical agreement. "Roscoe, I've

never known you to share anything, least of all a willing woman. Were you, perhaps, hit by a mail coach while I was away?"

"Nothing of the sort," Roscoe replied, once again in a pique over having his intentions questioned. "I thought you might like the opportunity, especially when the word all over Town is that your mother has your bride and nursery at the ready."

Kingsley flinched. Gads, he'd hoped that part of his life wasn't being bandied about, but here was Augie, looking away and whistling, and Roscoe grinning confidently over the news.

Yes, it was all over Town.

"Not interested," he told his old friend, for certainly there was some hitch in all this.

It was Roscoe doing the offering after all.

"Now, now, now. Wait until you behold the lady before you refuse this choice opportunity," Roscoe said, catching him by the arm and turning him toward the open garden doors. "See the milkmaid there, lingering as if she hadn't a single concern about her flock or her virtue?"

Against his better judgment, Kingsley looked.

He should never have done so.

Even Augie gasped, for indeed, the lady near the doors was the loveliest creature Kingsley had beheld in a very long time. Long hair fell in curls all the way down her back. Her gown, rather than the usual fluff and frills of some noble version of a milkmaid, was instead simple and classical, a soft sheath of muslin tied at her waist with a single silken cord.

A plain white mask covered the upper half of her face, but

beneath it were a pair of pink, full lips that right now she was nibbling with her teeth.

Kingsley blinked even as his body tightened. Yes, this was exactly what he'd had in mind to discover.

More to the point, however had he missed her before this?

She was Sheba with a shepherdess's crook.

Demmit, what man wouldn't want her?

"What is the wager?" Kingsley said, taking a step toward her.

"A monkey," Roscoe told him. "And of course, the pleasure of her company."

"Kingsley, I wouldn't—" Augie began, but was quickly overshadowed by Roscoe, who had clapped his hand over Augie's mouth and shoved Augie behind him.

"Should I put your name down?" Roscoe asked, all innocence.

"Ah," Kingsley said with a grin. "Why not."

"Kingsley—no—" Augie struggled to get free, but it was too late, for the major was already striding confidently off through the press of guests.

Roscoe waited until their friend was well out of earshot, then began to laugh. Uproariously.

"Badly done," Augie scolded, coming round him and watching in dismay as Kingsley made his approach. "Do you know who that lady really is?"

"Of course I do," Roscoe said with glee.

"He'll call you out when he discovers what you've done," Augie pointed out. "Years of practice aiming at those wily Frogs . . . you'll make an easy target in comparison."

"Hadn't thought of that," Roscoe admitted, making a noncommittal shrug, but nonetheless taking an uneasy glance at Kingsley.

"You never do, Roscoe," Augie replied. "You never do."

"Ah, fair milkmaid," came a rich, deep voice off to Lady Arabella Tremont's right.

Fair milkmaid. How original. She nearly sighed. For she knew what would come next. The comparisons of her eyes to sapphires. How her hair was a river of honeyed chestnut. Her form that of a . . .

With this being her fourth Season out, she'd heard every compliment, every greeting men seemed capable of offering. Was there a single man in London who didn't steal his lines of besotted admiration from the same tired book of poetry?

When she turned around she knew what she would find—some costumed blade who might be mildly handsome. He'd have come this way to claim her hand because he was "madly in love with her," but what he was madly in love with was the prospect of her dowry, that and being married to the Duke of Parkerton's only daughter.

So it was each time she attended a ball, a soiree, some costumed fête. There was nothing about tonight that hinted that this encounter would be any different.

Yet when she did turn, her dull, predictable world tilted. Before her stood a tall, plainly dressed gentleman—wearing what could hardly be called a costume, just an unassuming black jacket, breeches, and a simple half mask—yet there was nothing simple about this man.

His bearing came with a sense of power, strength, as if he

expected his every wish, his every command to be answered. From the breadth of his shoulders, to the way they tapered down to a narrow waist, to his long limbs and the set of his solid jaw, everything about him drew her eye—such raw masculinity couldn't have been hidden by any costume.

Certainly his plain drapings only accentuated the wide expanse between him and his preening counterparts. Set him on a commanding pedestal all his own.

A height that left him able to let his gaze rake over her with an intimacy, a claiming that had her wishing for her wrap.

Good heavens, it was as if the man was imagining her naked.

Naked, indeed! Now she was the one being ridiculous. For next he'd offer some well-practiced endearments, a bit of poetry, some offer to guess who she was, when the fellow knew very well who she was.

Everyone did. Oh, to be an anonymous miss with a world of possibilities before her.

"Lovely milkmaid," he continued as he bowed slightly, and with daring presumption caught her hand in his steely grasp and pulled her close, so he might whisper in her ear. A smooth, quick sally that left her unable to protest.

For he was doing what no other man had ever dared—breaching the high, proper walls that were her due as an heiress and the pampered daughter of a duke. Why, the rogue was peeling her glove off with a slow deliberateness, as if it was common practice to remove a lady's glove.

In full view of the entire ballroom.

That, and his breath was teasing over the shell of her ear in a most delicious way, leaving her feeling a bit light-headed.

Her! Lady Arabella Tremont. The girl who'd been thrown out of Miss Emery's School for being too bold.

Not to be undone by his brazen manners, she straightened and did her best to appear unruffled and uninterested in what this rake had to say.

Or do.

Save his touch was sending the most dangerous and teasing tendrils of desire through her.

This was desire, wasn't it? Was this what it was like to be seduced?

Well, there was one thing to be said for this rogue—he was very good at it. Because as her glove slid from her hand, she had the outlandish irritation that he was taking much too long to remove it.

"I have heard your praises sung daily since I returned to London," he was saying.

"You have?" she replied, looking around for her father. This was exactly the sort of thing he was always railing on about—and she couldn't make up her mind if she wanted his intervention or for the duke to be well out of the way.

"Certainly," he told her, a slow grin lighting up his smooth, hard lips, while behind his mask, his eyes twinkled with mischief. "And none of the tributes were exaggerated. For even from across the room, your lips drew me closer. And now there is nothing I would love more, my dear milkmaid, than for you to wrap them around my cock tonight, and when you are finished, I promise I shall return the favor and devour the rest of your delicious and notable delights until you can't even remember your name."

Arabella's mouth fell open.

Had he just said what she thought he'd said?

He wanted her to do what?

Worse, he took her gaping as some sort of acquiescence on her part, or perhaps just an early offer, for he steered her out the open garden doors before she could manage a protest.

She stole a glance up at him and there behind his mask was a smoky light of sensuality—after four Seasons she wasn't so innocent that she didn't know what *that* meant.

Worse yet, it sent a tremor of desire, a rare curiosity down her limbs. His cock aside, whatever had he meant, that he'd devour her in return?

Just considering the notion sent a delicious shiver down her spine. Especially when she looked at his full, strong lips. Which, she guessed, would be only the beginning of what was strong and firm about him.

Oh, good heavens, she shouldn't even be thinking such things. Considering such notions. Then again, no man, no one, had ever spoken to her thusly.

And Arabella, for the first time in her life, was at a loss as to what to say in return.

While she knew what she should do—protest loudly and send him off with a sharp, stinging retort—at that moment, he pulled her close, and the desire in his eyes, a mesmerizing light, left her once again wavering as her world took an unfamiliar tilt.

Not even the realization that she was far deeper in the gardens than she ought to be, or that she was up against him, his arm wound intimately around her waist, gave her the wherewithal to panic properly. For there was one undeniable truth that held her in place.

He was indeed strong. And very firm.

Yet this time when he spoke, it had the opposite effect, his words breaking the passionate spell he'd cast. "My lovely Mrs. Spenser—"

Mrs. Who?

Then the name came to her. *Mrs. Spenser.* "You cannot think—"

"Oh, dear Vestal, I can think a lot of things. Like how I've discovered you first. Which I understand has earned me a perfect night."

"A perfect wha-a-at?"

"A perfect night in your bed, isn't that so?" He grinned again, this time wickedly, and much to Arabella's horror, it only made him that much more distracting.

Then, to make matters worse, he began nibbling on her earlobe, whispering a litany of ways he was going to make her night memorable.

"I . . . I . . . I hardly think—" she stammered to protest. But all too quickly it became clear she wasn't going to be able to think for much longer. Suddenly she was drowning in wave after wave of the most distracting suggestions . . . and sensations.

Oh, heaven help her! Whatever was he doing with his tongue?

Truly, he should cease such improprieties immediately.

Or very soon.

"No, no, you needn't protest," he whispered, his breath hot and warm in delicious contrast to the cool breeze in the garden. "Perhaps you need references. A hint of what is to come?" His hand slid up from her waist and cupped her breast, his fingers quickly finding her nipple and teasing it into a hard point

"I don't think . . . Oh, my!" she gasped. His touch left her spiraling, falling even as she rose up on her tiptoes. She couldn't help herself. His touch, his lips were heaven, guiding her, pulling her toward something she'd only imagined.

"I promise, I will surprise you," he whispered in a deep, husky voice.

Arabella blinked and tried to make sense of what was happening. Truly, he needn't promise such a thing. He'd already made good on that pledge.

She was utterly surprised. No, make that shocked.

"All that is left to do is slip off that mask of yours, so I can see the beauty that has all of London in your thrall," he said, as his fingers reached behind her head to untangle the ties holding it in place. "Tomorrow morning, after I've discovered every delectable, delightful corner of your divine body, will you perhaps tell me what happened to Mr. Spenser?"

Mr. Spenser? There had been a Mr. Spenser? Arabella couldn't help herself, she smiled. That was quite contradictory to what Lady Davinia had claimed the other day at her mother's afternoon in.

They call themselves Mrs. This or Mrs. That, but there never was a "mister." None whatsoever, Davinia had told her avid audience. And Lady Davinia would know. Her brother was the worst sort of libertine.

At least that was what Aunt Josephine had said at the breakfast table the next morning. She might have said more on the subject if Papa hadn't *shushed* her.

Mr. Spenser! Oh, wouldn't it be wonderful to steal a

march on that gossipy Lady Davinia and tell her there *was* a Mr. Spenser.

Meanwhile, her erstwhile seducer was continuing to outline his plans for their evening, while his fingers did their best to untie her mask.

As he described his sensual ambitions for the hours to come, starting with how he was going to remove her gown, Arabella's eyes widened and her mouth fell open.

Such things were possible? And here she'd always thought that book Thalia Langley had passed around Miss Emery's had been naught but French nonsense.

Yet here was this gentleman offering to do exactly that and more.

More so, from the look in his eye. The odd shiver that ran down her spine all the way to that spot between her legs at the very thought of such intimacy made Arabella realize it must be *very* possible.

And *very* pleasurable.

In that instant, she saw the man before her naked—well, she could imagine *that*. She had, after all, seen the Elgin Marbles. But now she saw that perfect masculine form in a new light. In the flesh, warm and hot, covering her, his lips caressing her skin, his tongue sliding over her, leaving a heated, wet trail, until he came right down to her . . .

"Oh, my heavens," she whispered as her body tingled with a dangerous anticipation.

He'd finished untying the knot and was slowly working the strings away from her carefully arranged hairdo. "Come now, Mrs. Spenser, don't be coy with me. However can you blush so—when I have no doubt you are as eager to see if I can hold up my end of the bargain as I am to prove it." With that, he caught hold of her hand and was about to place it on his . . .

No, not there. . .

Arabella snatched her fingers back and found her voice. "Sir! What is wrong with you? I am not Mrs. Spenser!"

Even as she said the words, he had succeeded in freeing her mask and it fell away, leaving her face bared for him, her identity his to discover.

Whatever he saw, whatever he'd expected to find, it obviously wasn't she. His eyes widened and then he hastily ripped off his own mask to get a better look. And if the way his expression changed from darkly smoky to shocked was any indication, he had all too quickly realized his mistake.

"Who the devil are you?" His tone overflowed with censure. As if this was entirely her fault.

Arabella's temper rose as quickly as her passions had. "Me? I can tell you who I am not. Some Incognita to be bartered and bandied with."

His eyes darkened and he looked back over his shoulder toward the ballroom. "That bastard. When I get my hands on him—"

She caught hold of his sleeve and gave it a tug to regain his attention. "I think you should be apologizing to *me*, not looking for someone else to molest," she huffed. "Why, of all the common sort of ruffians I've had the misfortune to meet—"

Truly, she'd never met one, but he didn't know that.

Yet Arabella wasn't done with him. "I suspect even Mrs. Spenser would find you beneath her."

His wolfish expression returned in a flash. "I had had rather high hopes of finding her just so—"

Against her better judgment, she silently finished the implication he'd made.

Beneath me.

But it wasn't the courtesan that Arabella saw beneath this man, but herself. Naked and willing. His touch had left her shivering, the brush of his lips leaving her to feel a beggar in his presence.

Take me beneath you, a very devilish part of her wanted to plead.

Instead, she folded her arms across her chest, tamping her desires back into the confines where they belonged. "You, sir, are most certainly not a gentleman."

"If I'm not a gentleman, what does that make you? I will point out, you came quite willingly with me. What sort of milkmaid comes out to the gardens when a gentleman asks her to—?"

"Oh, please do not repeat yourself!" she told him. "Do not ask me such a thing ever again!"

"Oh, please do," came another voice. A deep and very familiar one. "I would like to know what you asked my daughter to do."

But her swain had no time to answer, because the Duke of Parkerton followed up his question by spinning the man around, and then landing a hard-fisted blow that left the devilish fellow in a heap on the ground, out cold.

CHAPTER 2

The next morning, Arabella stood by the window in the breakfast room awaiting her reckoning. Papa hadn't said a word the entire way home from the Setchfield ball, which meant the explosion was only a matter of time.

The Duke of Parkerton was known for his reckonings. After all, he'd had years of experience calling to heel his younger brother, Lord John, known throughout the *ton* as "Mad Jack."

And she had a sense of what this particular reckoning would be. He'd finally have all the ammunition he needed to marry her off to the Duke of Marbury's heir.

All of it for her "own good."

Behind her, her stepmother, Elinor, and Elinor's young sister, Tia, sat eating their breakfast.

"Come and have a bit of toast, Birdie," Tia called out, using Arabella's nickname. "Everything is always better with a bit of toast and jam."

"Yes, please do join us," Elinor urged her. "Afterward, we are planning a walk in the park with James. You'd like that, wouldn't you?"

She actually would—she loved her new little brother. The heir that Elinor had provided the Duke of Parkerton within a year of their marriage. No one had been more surprised than the duke himself to become a father again. And if Arabella was to venture a guess, a spare would make an appearance not long after Michaelmas if the bulge in Elinor's usually trim figure was any indication.

Not that Arabella minded in the least seeing her family expand—especially given her father's happiness in the three years since he'd married Elinor after a madcap and scandalous courtship. Even better, little James's arrival had become the perfect distraction to keep her father from pressing her to marry—well, that is, *marry well*.

Still, despite Elinor and her sister's friendly pleas, Arabella continued to hold her place by the window. She couldn't eat. Not yet. Not until this reckoning with her father was over. His silence in the carriage home had nearly been her undoing.

Aunt Josephine, who sat in her usual spot at the table, winked at Arabella, and then went back to eating her breakfast. Most likely her elderly relation knew every detail of the night's events.

Then out in the garden, the gate opened and the milkmaid came through, right on schedule, carrying the day's delivery. As always, she arrived whistling a dashing tune, the bright notes carried along on a morning breeze.

Elinor's ever-present dogs, Fagus and Isadore, sat up and began barking at this intruder, racing in circles around the table and yapping as if the hordes of London had descended on their garden.

While outside, the girl, used to the dogs' ambitious greetings each morning, smiled as if her burdens and their yapping threats were nothing to concern her, and Arabella let out a sigh of envy.

"What is it?" Tia asked, twisting around to look out the window. "Oh, it's her."

"Every morning she comes through our gate, bringing us those buckets of milk."

"They look heavy," Tia said in her very practical way and returned to her breakfast.

"They do indeed," Arabella agreed, "and yet she smiles and whistles. Whistles!"

Arabella couldn't whistle. Not a note, and a rare whisper of envy moved through her heart.

She wondered if the maid had a fellow who caught her in his arms and whispered into her ear as Arabella's unknown swain had the night before.

Did the maid's knees shiver together at the thought of him touching her as that rogue had promised Arabella last night?

Did the milkmaid let him?

Was it as wickedly wonderful as those brief teasing moments had hinted? Arabella wondered.

"There she is," Arabella remarked, as the girl came back into view. "She's always as happy as a lark."

"Perhaps she is happy because her buckets are empty," Tia pointed out.

"I don't think her burdens weigh all that heavily on her," Arabella said, unable to keep the wistful note out of her words.

"I think you spend far too much time looking out the

window," Tia remarked as she plucked another piece of toast from the rack.

"That's it exactly!" Arabella said, leaving the window and coming to a stop behind her chair. Her chair. The one she always sat in. Everything about her life was like that. The same routine, the same people, the very same entertainments day after day, year after year, and she, Lady Arabella Tremont, was miserable. Out in the garden, the gate was swinging shut. "She wears the same dress—homespun, I imagine— and the same shabby boots, and yet she's happy." She glanced at Tia and Elinor. "Happy! How is that?"

"I don't know," Elinor said, smiling up at her. She looked ready to say more, but someone else joined the conversation.

"Perhaps she's content with her lot in life." This came from the doorway and they all turned to find the duke standing there. He paused for only a moment and then came in, first placing a gentle, lingering kiss upon his wife's forehead, and then taking his place at the head of the table. "Your milkmaid is content because she knows her place."

Arabella shook her head. "No, Papa. She's happy because she's free."

"Freedom is a rare commodity for a lady," Elinor remarked.

"If I were free for just one day—" Arabella began.

"You? Free?" Her father began to laugh. "If you were set free you'd be in the suds before you crossed the street." He shook out his napkin. "You, free! What utter nonsense."

"James—" Elinor began, but was cut off by her husband.

"Arabella Tremont," the duke said, having warmed to his subject and still furious from the night before, "you have more freedom than any milkmaid. You want for nothing and yet all you want is more."

"I never asked for any of this," she shot back, waving her hand at the gilt room and the overladen sideboard, as if it was all a burden to be borne, heavier and more unwieldy than the milkmaid's buckets.

"No one does," he told her. "That is why it is called 'your lot in life.' And you had best wed yourself to the notion that your lot doesn't involve dashing about alleyways like a common milkmaid, nor does it involve kissing every scalawag and bit of riffraff who comes along."

"He kissed you?" Tia exclaimed, eyes wide with shock.

"He kissed you?!" Aunt Josephine said, but her statement rang with surprise and delight. Suddenly, she perked up and grinned at the Arabella, eagerly awaiting the details.

Oh, bother, this was Aunt Josephine. She'd demand the details.

"Certainly not!" she shot back—for all their sakes—even as the color rose on her cheeks to be reminded of what had transpired. "He didn't kiss me."

If one didn't count what he'd done to the spot behind her ear. She'd lain awake a good part of the night caught in memory of that delicious moment.

Yet he hadn't kissed her. Much to Arabella's chagrin. But he'd done enough that she'd discovered a different kind of freedom.

In his touch. In the way he'd teased her into a breathless state.

Awakened her.

Without even kissing her.

"That's rather disappointing," Aunt Josephine declared, and went back to her breakfast.

The duke shot his great-aunt a scathing glance—which was a complete waste of time, for nothing and no one had ever managed to quell Lady Josephine Tremont. After a moment, he turned his wrath back on his rebellious daughter. "The only reason you aren't ruined and the headline of every gossip column in London is because I found you in time."

"Gossip columns!" Arabella scoffed. "You've always told me to ignore their prattle. As it is, I've never read them, and expect nor does anyone who is of consequence or good manners."

At this, Aunt Josephine snapped her paper shut and set it aside, taking a renewed interest in her breakfast.

"Good manners, indeed!" The duke followed this pronouncement with a loud *harrumph*. "Being free with your manners is how that devil managed to get you out into that garden in the first place."

"You went out in the garden with him?" Now Tia was shocked. Then again, she was newly returned from Miss Emery's School in Bath and had graduated with a very strict sense of what a lady did and what a lady *never* did.

Lessons Arabella had missed because she'd been thrown out after only a year.

For kissing the stable hand . . .

Not that she'd had a chance to kiss anyone else since.

Her father had seen to that.

Still, looking from her father's outraged expression to Tia's one of horror, Arabella knew she needed to explain. "He took me outside because he thought I was—"

She stopped herself right there. Telling her father that this rogue had mistaken her for one of London's most infamous courtesans would hardly be a point in her favor.

He probably wouldn't let her out of the house for the rest of the Season.

Nor was the duke about to let her lapse lay fallow. "Who did he think you were?"

She wasn't a Tremont for nothing. Arabella stood her ground and refused to yield.

Or rather, condemn herself.

"He thought I was someone else," she said, chin tucked up defiantly. "And I wish I was." With that, she got up and fled.

Because more humiliating than having her father give an accounting of her scandalous evening was the memory of it.

Oh, bother! Arabella wished that rogue had kissed her. Just once. Maybe twice.

Wished with all her heart, her unknown seducer had given her the taste of freedom she so craved. Desired with all her heart.

And now, would never know.

"**S**he is just like her mother," James Lambert St. Maur Thurstan Tremont, the ninth Duke of Parkerton, told his wife an hour later when Elinor joined him in his study.

Elinor said nothing and sat down in the chair near the fireplace. She nodded toward the one opposite hers.

Parkerton rose from his desk and joined her, though he preferred to hold such discussions with the wide expense of his imposing desk before him like a stern buffer. For years it had been his brother, Jack, standing across from him and enduring another lecture. Now it seemed all his "discussions" were about Arabella.

"She is going to that house party," he said, knowing he sounded like a stubborn old mule. But he saw no other way to keep his daughter from making a disastrous mistake.

"Wasn't her mother forced to marry a man she didn't love?" Elinor pointed out in that quiet, yet firm way of hers.

Parkerton pressed his lips together and shifted in his chair. Damn his wife and her penchant for pointing out the obvious.

Which he also supposed was why he'd fallen in love with her.

Nor was Elinor done. "And when you discovered your wife had loved another, hadn't wanted to marry you, how did that make you feel? I know how I felt when I was forced to wed a man I didn't love."

He glanced away for he didn't want to answer that. And demmit if Elinor wasn't right most of the time. Oh, bother, demmed near always.

"Whyever do you want to consign Arabella to the same fate?" his wife pressed. That they had both had terrible first marriages, and yet been able to overcome all that grief and find each other, was something of a miracle to them both.

Since it was no comfort to Parkerton that he wasn't going to win the day by forcing Arabella, he changed course a bit. "She refuses to even meet Marbury's heir. She is being overly stubborn and willful."

He did his best to ignore how stubborn and willful his declaration sounded.

Elinor didn't. "Do you blame her? What with you and

his father pushing for this match with every breath. It is a wonder she and Somersale haven't conspired together to have you both tossed in the Thames."

"She merely has to meet the fellow," Parkerton asserted, ignoring his own stubbornly held desires.

Elinor wasn't about to ignore them. She threw up her hands and chided him. "You'll push her too far and she'll make some disastrous choice."

He shook his head. "Her mother didn't. She knew her duty. Her lot in life."

"Her mother may have been resigned to her 'lot in life,' as you call it, but Arabella is half Tremont." Elinor's brow arched upward and she needn't say any more.

After all, that half is what kept Parkerton awake most nights in a dead panic.

A sennight later, Arabella followed her father down the front steps of the house, as if being led toward her own hanging. The staff, all lined up as they always were when her father departed, watched the proceedings with woeful expressions.

The invitation to the Duke of Marbury's house party had been accepted and she was being led off to meet and consent to a suitable marriage partner.

No more strangers in the gardens for Arabella. No more suitors. No more whispered promises in the moonlight.

She was to be wed, and that was the end of the matter.

Near the front of the line, their faithful and beloved housekeeper burst into tears. "The poor little lamb," she managed through the sobs before she pressed her apron to her face.

Arabella rushed forward and gave her a hug. "There, there, Mrs. Oxton, it isn't like I won't be coming home."

Hopefully she'd get a chance to come home before . . . Before she was married off to Marbury's heir like a prized filly, all bloodlines and proper matches and not a single consideration of love or passion.

Decidedly not passion.

Now it was Arabella's turn to give a bit of a sniff. It wasn't really like she was crying, not until she glanced over at their butler.

Even Cantley, dear, dour Cantley, looked ready to dash aside a sheen of moisture in his eyes. "My lady, sweet Birdie, be brave," he said quietly.

Arabella felt the depths of her mortification run all the way down to the tips of her traveling boots and then turned her gaze toward the single person responsible: her father.

Her glare of accusation was followed by the eyes of all the servants. And they in turn added their own scowls.

The duke shifted uncomfortably, for ever since his marriage to Elinor, and a bit before, there had been a revolution of sorts among his staff that had left the household united in their opinions.

And not always in the duke's favor.

"Come now," Parkerton said, sounding nothing like a father but entirely like a duke, nodding toward the open door of the carriage with a curt tip of his head.

Taking a deep breath, Arabella notched her chin up, appearing as brave as she could, as she made her way to the carriage, taking her cue from Aunt Josephine, who always strode through life as if she were a queen without a care.

She climbed into the carriage, reminded herself it wasn't a tumbrel, as much as it felt like one, and sat in the seat opposite Aunt Josephine.

Behind her, Tia followed carrying Fagus. As usual, the little terrier was ready for an adventure, barking and twisting in the younger girl's grasp, and notably the only one eager to be starting out. "Oh, Fagus, do be still!" the girl scolded.

"Haven't you ever wanted to just slip your leash," Aunt Josephine remarked as Tia settled into the seat next to her. "If not for just a day?" Her eyes were alight with mischief as she echoed the very same sentiment that had gotten Arabella in so much trouble with her father.

If only she could . . .

And then it happened.

Fagus slipped from Tia's grasp—slipped or prodded loose, who could say?—and the little dog was off and out of the carriage in a flash.

In an instant, Arabella's world erupted into chaos—Elinor calling out in distress, Parkerton barking orders to catch that wretched beast, and the servants dashing to and fro trying to be the first to apprehend the escapee.

Only Aunt Josephine remained calmly in her seat, smiling at Arabella, and more notably at the open and unguarded door of the carriage.

And there was something about the sight of Fagus's expression as he'd made his unlikely escape, the unfettered look of joy as he'd jumped from his captivity, that snapped the invisible cords that bound Arabella's life into a tight knot.

Like the wry notes of the milkmaid's song, Arabella once again saw the bright light of freedom.

"Go."

She never did know if it was Aunt Josephine who whispered that command or some long-held magic inside her, but *go* is exactly what Arabella did.

She dashed out of the carriage, in much the same madcap fashion as Fagus, and then came to a blinding stop.

It was one thing to be free, but what then?

She glanced up to find Mrs. Oxton nodding at her.

But when Cantley spotted her, the old man panicked. He was about to cry out, but his alarm ended in a great *whoosh* as Mrs. Oxton rammed her elbow into his ribs.

The housekeeper pointed down the block, in the opposite direction that Fagus had gone, and Arabella didn't hesitate; she dashed away from Cavendish Square and hurried into the teeming streets of London beyond. Three blocks away, she was still running blindly, bolting into the street in front of a fast-moving curricle.

The carriage and horses came to a clattering, shuddering halt, the horses' breath hot against her face where she stood frozen in place.

"I say, what is the matter with you?" the driver shouted, rising up in his seat.

That voice stopped her flight cold. Arabella's heart, which had nearly stopped as well, began to pound. Furiously.

Slowly, she tipped her chin up to look out from beneath the brim of her bonnet so she could see his face.

Him.

Though she'd really only glimpsed his face that night, she'd never forget that strong jaw, nor his commanding height. Like he'd been at the ball, he was dressed plainly, today in a driving coat and buff breeches. Even his cravat was knotted into nothing more than a simple mail coach.

Still, she found herself mesmerized. For all she had dreamt of him every night since the ball, now all the pieces—from his blazing eyes, his high cheekbones and carved jaw—tumbled together.

It startled her to realize he was even more handsome than she'd dared imagine.

As she tipped back the brim of her poke bonnet, his eyes widened. "You!"

Though it hardly sounded like a happy greeting, it was enough for Arabella.

Taking his recognition as an invitation, she hurried around the horses and then climbed up into the seat beside him.

He gaped at her in shock. Evidently he wasn't that much of a rake, for the unexpected arrival of a lady in his carriage had left him at a loss.

So she gave him the prompt he needed. "Whatever are you waiting for? Drive, will you?"

Arabella settled back in the seat, hands folded properly in her lap. She glanced over at her still dumbfounded Sir Galahad and nodded at the street before them. "If you don't mind. I'm in a bit of a hurry."

For couldn't he see, all of London lay before them.

CHAPTER 3

"In a hurry? The only place I'm taking you is to your home."
Kingsley glanced around to see if anyone was going to come
collect her.

Like the wardens from Bedlam.

"I'm not going there." She made her declaration as if she
had underlined it. "I've only just left."

Only just left, *or* been cast out, he wondered.

"Oh, yes, you are," he shot back as he picked up the reins,
again looking around the crowded street and spying no one
who appeared to be looking for an errant miss. "I don't fancy
another run-in with that bruiser who left me in half mourn-
ing." He turned his head toward her so she could see the last
remnants of the black eye he'd been sporting since the Setchfield ball.

"The bruiser would be my father," she supplied, her eyes
widening as she looked directly at him. "Oh, dear! Did he do
that?"

"If he was the one who floored me, then yes, he did."

"I'm so terribly sorry," she replied, her hand reaching up

to touch his cheek, but just before her fingers grazed over the tender spot, she pulled her hand back. "I fear he has a devil of a temper. Or so my aunt always says."

Devil of a temper, indeed! The man should be in the boxing circuit. Might well be, for all Kingsley knew. That thought gave him both pause and the resolve to wash his hands of this vexing bit of muslin as quickly as he could.

"I'm taking you home," he told her. Or at the very least, dropping her off on the nearest corner, since he didn't relish another encounter with her father nor the thought of a matching black eye.

"Home?" Her eyes immediately began to well up and her lower lip quivered. "No, no. I beg of you, don't make me go there. I won't." Then the lady burst into tears.

Oh, hell! Not tears. Anything but tears.

"I'm . . . I'm . . . hardly prone to such . . . such . . . displays," she sobbed. "But I've never run away from home before. Or had to ask for aid from a stranger."

"We are hardly strangers," he teased, if only to get her to stop crying. Sadly, his remark prodded on a new river of tears down her cheeks. "Oh, good Lord," he muttered as she dug around unsuccessfully in her reticule for a handkerchief, her sniffles and sobs continuing unabated. He reached into his pocket and found his, giving it to her.

Yet when she blew her nose, he regretted his gallantry immediately, for he wasn't positive he had another one packed in his valise.

"Do stop," he implored as she made another loud, messy noise into the confines of his once perfectly clean handkerchief.

"I cannot." The chit sobbed anew. "My life is a horrible mess."

"How horrible can it be?"

Her tears, most thankfully, took a respite for a moment as she considered her next lament. And when she began, her words tumbled out in a steady stream, much like her sobs. "My father is forcing me into a marriage with ... with ..." The tears overtook her again.

"It can hardly be as bad—"

"—and it is all your fault," she managed to sputter.

That stopped him. "My fault?"

"Yes," she blurted out, along with another sob. "If you hadn't ... That is ... When you ..." Her cheeks blushed deeply.

"If I hadn't what?" he demanded. He damned well knew what she meant. Hell, he had the last vestiges of a black eye to prove his part in all of it.

His little nemesis huffed loudly, with all the air of a duchess, and went back to wiping her nose.

With his handkerchief.

"If you hadn't done what you did the other night—" she declared, once again all lofty airs, "my father wouldn't be forcing me to marry—" She stopped there, not naming her intended, as if she'd realized in that instance that a single name would be all the clue he needed to deliver her up ... somewhere, anywhere, anyplace other than in his company.

And whoever the poor devil was, Kingsley said a hasty prayer for the fellow. Still he had to ask, "How bad can he be?"

"Oh, heavens! He's a dreadful beast!"

Kingsley was glad for the clarification. Especially since

that covered a good part of London's male population. Still he couldn't help asking—and teasing a bit—"How dreadful?"

"He's old," she said, shuddering as if the cold hand of death was upon her. "At least thirty."

"Decrepit," Kingsley agreed, trying not to laugh. With his own thirtieth birthday only a month away, she most likely would declare him Methuselah's closest relation.

"Exactly," she said, brightening noticeably, having warmed to her subject. "And horribly dull."

"Why not tell this old, horribly dull fellow you don't want to marry him?"

"How can I?" She heaved another sigh. "I've never met him."

Kingsley stilled. "You've never met him?"

"No." She hadn't looked up at him when she'd whispered that one word. As if she were embarrassed of the truth. "And there is no avoiding the matter, my father has made that clear."

She was being sacrificed to the altar of marriage—without any choice, without any say in the matter.

A humiliation he knew only too well. Wasn't he in much the same straits?

"That is why I had to leave," she continued, as if this alone was explanation enough. Yet when she turned her gaze up to his, her blue eyes brightened with an intensity, a resolute will as it were, to avoid her fate.

At any price.

A flicker of admiration lit inside him. She was doing exactly what he'd been threatening to do for nearly a month. Had done for the past three years.

But here he was, packed and ready to ride to the very fate

she was running away from. The irony of the situation didn't escape him, so when she nodded for him to drive on, he did.

As he guided the horses into the busy London traffic, Kingsley took a few furtive glances at his passenger. That night had been a bit of a blur, but this chit had left an indelible mark on his imagination.

The curve of her hip. The fullness of her breasts. The way she had fit against him. He'd awakened more than once in the past week, hot and hard, wondering how he could find her again.

Wondering if he dared . . .

Now here she was, dropped back into his grasp by Fate, with only one question prodding him. Who the devil was she?

No, make that two questions. For the second one rang just as loud.

Did he dare now that he had found her?

For one thing, she wasn't a waif. He knew enough about female rigging—having been dragged up and down Bond Street by his mother— to recognize his companion's gown and hat hadn't come cheap. They were the first stare, or so he would guess.

Why not just ask her name? a practical voice chided him.

If he was being honest, he supposed he didn't want to know who she was—for it hardly mattered. His path and hers had already been decided.

Still he couldn't help sneaking another searching glance in her direction, but this time found her doing her own reconnaissance.

"Do you ever long to be free?" she asked in that bluntly direct manner of hers.

More so, her question took him aback. As did his answer, for it sprang up before he could stop himself. "Always."

Especially now. With the war over, his travels completed, there were no more excuses he could make to avoid his destiny.

Yet apparently, she didn't believe him. "You have no idea what I mean." She sniffed and crossed her arms over chest.

"Enlighten me." Kingsley only asked because the more she talked, the less she cried. And then he wouldn't be out two handkerchiefs.

That, and he clung to the hope she'd slip up and tell him enough about herself or her family so he could take her home.

"You can go wherever you please, can you not?" she asked.

"Of course."

"As you please?"

"Yes." A twinge of guilt pricked at him. His answer wasn't entirely true. For here he was going home.

Make that *summoned.*

"To Astley's? Or to Vauxhall Gardens? Even Bond Street shopping?"

"I suppose, if I wanted to go to those places." He had no problem being honest there.

She failed to notice his disdain. "Yes, of course you can. Men can go wherever they like. Whereas I cannot."

"You seemed quite at home the other night in that ball-room," he pointed out. *And in the garden as well. . .*

"The Setchfield masquerade ball, bah!" She shuddered as if it had been an afternoon in a parlor full of gossipy tabbies. "How many times must we all be horrified by the sight of Lady Blundstone done up as Venus?"

Well, there was no arguing that point. Yet he paused for a second, like a bird picking at crumbs. Here was a hint as to who she might be. She knew Lady Blundstone.

Yet that was hardly a defining connection. Everyone in London knew Lady Blundstone—it was often joked that Gillray himself had modeled most of his buxom bawds after the baroness.

Kingsley worked his jaw back and forth. However was he going to determine who this minx was, short of rattling it out of her?

Meanwhile, she continued to prattle on about her plight. "Do you know, I've never had a single day to myself. Not one. How fair is that?"

"I can't believe you've never—"

"Never!" she shot back. "My father dictates every facet of my day. Do this. Don't go there. Accept this invitation." She shuddered and glanced away. "My life has never been my own."

On that, Kingsley could sympathize wholeheartedly. Wasn't it very similar to arguments he'd made to his father just a fortnight ago?

How can you insist upon this marriage? I'm the one who will be saddled with this chit for the rest of my days, not you.

Meanwhile, the pretty little mystery beside him continued on. "Why should the milkmaid have every bit of freedom she desires, when I have none?"

A milkmaid. Kingsley's imagination got the better of him and he thought back to that night. When she'd been a very fetching sort of milkmaid. "You mean you aren't one?" he teased.

"No, of course not," she said, shaking her head at this foolishness, but he didn't miss the hint of smile on her pretty lips.

Still, he had to ask, "Whatever has a milkmaid to do with all this?"

"Everything," she said, as if that made the entire conversation quite clear. Nor was she done with her lament. "Am I so different from a milkmaid?"

This made him smile. *In about a thousand different ways. . .*

"Our milkmaid whistles. I don't even know how."

"To milk a cow?" he continued to tease, hoping to see that smile again.

"No, you widgeon," she said, swatting him on the arm. "To whistle."

He glanced at her and laughed. "You can't whistle? Is that what all this is all about? Quite frankly, I was under the assumption that ladies weren't supposed to—"

"Bother what ladies are supposed to do!" she told him, swatting him again.

This time he rubbed his arm. She had the subtlety of a pugilist.

That should have been his first warning.

Along with her errant arrival into his life.

And a myriad of other details about her. When her mask had fallen free at the ball, he'd known immediately she wasn't some Incognita. The fresh, innocent—albeit furious—face that he'd found looking up at him had said all too clearly she wasn't who he'd thought.

Now, here in the daylight, she was even younger than he remembered, her features bright and rosy. And again, so very innocent.

So much so, when he recalled what he'd said to her that night in the garden, a solid shaft of mortification ran down his spine.

Good God, he'd asked this pretty minx to . . .

No, he didn't want to think about it.

Because worst of all, he still wanted her to . . . to touch him. Writhe naked beneath him. Put her lips on him and kiss him deeply. Everywhere.

Whatever was it about her that left him hungry and hard? It had been that way the first moment he'd spied her at the ball, and now, as he sat next to her, a hint of her perfume teasing his senses, a rising desire to take her in his arms and finish what he'd started that night seemed capable of undoing his best intentions.

Oh, but that air of innocence about her stopped him. And the longer he remained in her company, he knew without a doubt, the more complicated matters would become.

Not that his life wasn't already all tangled up in knots of obligations. Including his own marriage plight. But as much as he could sympathize with her, he could see that there was only one thing he could do. Only one choice to be made.

Kingsley pulled the carriage to a stop. "Who are you? A name, or I won't drive another foot."

Her chin notched up, defiantly so. Worse, there was a wobble to that chin, and her eyes appeared to be welling up again.

His heart sank. No, that wouldn't do. He was certain he didn't have another handkerchief—at least not one at the ready—and he wasn't sure the one she had wound up in her hand could take another flood of tears.

There was a gulp and another sniffle. "Don't make me go back," she pleaded. "I can't abide the notion of marrying someone horrid. And old."

"He might be rich," Kingsley offered. In his experience that was often a deciding factor.

"Of course he's rich," she complained. "And titled. With a relic of a house."

"Sounds like a veritable ogre," he agreed, realizing she might be describing him—for he was all those things.

Save the old part.

She batted at him again, and he was starting to wonder if her father was Gentleman Jim. "Oh, do stop teasing me. I know I sound dreadfully selfish and spoiled. Which I might be."

"Might?" It was so easy to tease her ... And so tempting.

"But I didn't ask to be born the daughter of—" She glanced at him, her eyes wide with alarm as if she'd said too much. "Any more than you were born the—" She paused and looked him over. "Oh, dear, who are you exactly?"

"Your rescuer."

She sniffed. "Hardly, when you keep nattering on about taking me home."

Kingsley decided to make another run at discovering her secrets. "And where exactly is home?"

She wasn't fooled by his benign probing. "London."

"That hardly narrows it down."

"That is as narrow as it shall remain until I have my day. So you might as well set me down right now."

"I will deposit you somewhere—but only when I am assured you will be safe."

"I'd be safe right there," she said, pointing at the sidewalk where a trio of young blades stood. One of them winked at her, and another blew her a kiss. She straightened and looked away, a blush rising on her cheeks, telling him more about her than her half clues as to her identity. "Well, perhaps not there precisely."

"Let me get this straight," he began. "You think you can just go gallivanting through London on your own?"

"Why not?" Once again, her chin rose, her pert nose tipping up so very defiantly.

Oh, she was the devil's own, this one. He was starting to wonder, if he did find where she lived, if they would be willing to take her back.

She might have mistaken the matter and they'd actually let her go.

But that hardly solved his problem: What to do with her now? For just letting her go was out of the question.

"Why not?" he repeated. Kingsley could think of a thousand reasons "why not." "You'd be in trouble before you turned that corner." He nodded toward the intersection just up ahead.

Her brows shot up, as if taking his words not for the admonition that they were, but a challenge.

"That is ridiculous," she told him. "Whatever harm could befall me here?" She swept her hand regally over the landscape before them. "I might remind you we are in Mayfair."

He glanced up and saw for a moment what she most likely thought she was seeing—well-dressed matrons, proper maids, old Corinthians leaning over their canes, footmen hurrying to and fro on their errands.

Everything right and proper and well-ordered.

Except . . . she'd failed to notice the two urchins watching the crowd from the shadows of the nearby alleyway. The beggar woman weaving her way down the sidewalk—but to Kingsley's sharp eyes, she didn't appear to be a woman at all—not with those large hands and big feet. Then there were the two sharp-dressed culls leaning against the wall on the opposite side of the thoroughfare.

All of these seemingly innocent souls that his companion had blithely overlooked were seeking the same thing: a plump fool to pluck and pick like a lame pigeon.

"You don't believe me!" she sputtered, looking out over the same scene, oblivious to the dangers all around.

"No," he told her bluntly, as if that was the end of the discussion. The matter decided.

Which, he discovered very quickly, it wasn't. Before he could stop her, she gathered up her skirt and hopped down from the carriage.

"You just wait and see," she told him, hurrying through the traffic to the opposite sidewalk.

"Get back in this carriage," he ordered, only to have her wave him off and skip along, grinning at him when she made it to the other side.

See, I am perfectly safe.

At least she hadn't gone in the direction of the pair of sharpsters. Though her arrival hadn't gone unnoticed. But when one of them glanced up at him, Kingsley gave the fellow the most murderous gaze he could muster, and it was enough to send the pair skulking off down the street.

But in that moment, he also lost sight of her.

"Demmit," he cursed, getting to his feet and using the advantage of the curricle's height and his own imposing stance to see over the crowd. He couldn't even call for her, not when he didn't know her name.

But as he stood there, a litany of advice prodded at him.

Drive off.

Wash your hands of this.

You didn't ruin the gel. You don't owe her a demmed thing.

But he couldn't. He didn't know why—well, he did, but he wasn't about to consider such a foolish notion.

It wasn't as if he cared for her, as if she had been more than a flirtatious—albeit disastrous—moment at a ball.

Still, when her merry blue bonnet came into view like a beacon, and he spotted her in front of the bakeshop, he realized he'd been holding his breath, tensed and ready to pounce.

For a chit he barely knew.

Wanted nothing to do with. But he still couldn't shake his relief as he fixed his gaze on her slim figure standing before the shop window.

This looked harmless enough, he mused, relaxing his vigilant stance slightly. She'd get herself something to eat and then be back.

At least he thought that until he realized the two urchins he'd spied moments earlier were now making their way toward her.

And what unfolded next happened in the blink of an eye.

Like most of the trouble that happens in London.

Good heavens, Arabella thought as she jumped down from the carriage, he sounded as pompous as her father.

And as a duke, Arabella's father was the very definition of pompous—that is, according to her uncle Jack.

Nearly skipping with the heady air of freedom beneath her feet, she moved quickly to the other side of the street, sending a triumphant glance over her shoulder at *him*.

Then just as quickly glanced away. He rather towered above everyone else, and it wasn't just the curricle's height that gave him his lofty status. He was a tall, imposing figure of a man, and it made her shiver just to look at him.

Oh, there wasn't very much different about him—though in the daylight she could discern that his driving coat was of a very good wool and an excellent cut.

The sort of coat done by only the best, most exclusive of tailors.

So, who the devil was he? Having been in Society for the last four Seasons, she should have some inkling as to who he might be, but she hadn't the vaguest notion.

Worse, it didn't help that when she looked at him, her gaze strayed to his lips and she imagined what they might have felt like kissing her.

Oh, bother. That was exactly how young ladies of quality got into trouble. And she was determined to prove that she was capable of taking care of herself.

Which meant avoiding any entanglements that could be misconstrued. Yet here was her would-be rescuer glowering at the scene before him as if he thought she was wading through the plague.

Really, did he think her such a child to be chided and reminded how to walk in the street?! Though she hadn't any notion of what she was going to do next, certainly she wasn't about to be ruined on a street corner in Mayfair.

Not when the scent of freshly baked buns tickled at her nose. She turned in that direction.

A bakeshop. Arabella's stomach growled, a very unladylike noise, but one that reminded her that she hadn't eaten breakfast this morning.

Having never purchased anything in her life, she found it rather daring to walk right up to the woman, tray in hand, and ask, "One of those, if you please."

The woman glanced at her and then at her reticule.

Oh, yes, the coins. Arabella had almost forgotten. She fumbled with the strings and got out one of the pennies tucked inside and handed it over. "Will that do?"

"It will," the woman said, relinquishing one of the hot buns.

Triumph ran through her. Yet as she turned around to show her prize to her doubting Sir Galahad across the way, she found a small girl in a tattered dress in front of her.

"Excuse me, miss, but I haven't eaten in two days." The little urchin's grimy hand shot out and she looked up at Arabella with wide, sad brown eyes that implored for help.

"Oh, that's terrible," Arabella said, as she looked down at the poor forlorn little dear, her heart nearly breaking. Why, it appeared as if the child hadn't eaten in a week. She was so thin, and, dear heavens, shivering something terrible. "How very sad. You poor, poor thing."

"Could you—if it isn't too much . . ." The child glanced at the roll and then glanced down at the dirty cobbles as if the sight of the fresh baked roll was too much to hope for.

Behind Arabella, the mistress of the bakeshop snorted and picked up her laden tray, moving it out of reach.

That, she later realized, should have been her first indication that something was amiss.

And then she made her second mistake. Some might point out that this was her third error—if one counted that she should never have gotten out of the curricle.

But at that point her number of miscalculations was moot, for she handed over her breakfast.

Arabella would argue to her dying day that it hadn't been wrong to offer food to a starving child.

But a starving thief?

She held out the roll with both hands, leaning over to look the little girl in the eyes. In that instant, all the pretenses of suffering and agony fled from the child's face, replaced by a feral look of glee.

The roll left her hand in a flash, but so did her gloves, stripped off her hands in an instant. Even as she stumbled forward trying to retrieve them, she was bumped from behind and felt a jerk on her reticule strings.

Or rather where her reticule had been—cut from where it hung on her wrist. As she twisted around, she was able to spy a second slight figure loping off with his prize held in his greedy grasp.

"Oh, goodness, no!" she called out.

Realizing she couldn't catch him, she tried to snag the child closest to her, but that little urchin was ready for her. She caught hold of Arabella by the hand and spun her, shoving her in yet another direction, leaving her off balance.

And by the time she righted herself, both of the little miscreants were gone.

Behind her, she heard a carriage pulling to a stop.

"Had enough, or do you still think you can make it to the corner?" came the insolent query.

She cringed and then turned around, nose in the air. "Not one more word."

He didn't need words. He laughed. "Get in, you goose," he told her, scooting over to make room for her.

She glanced over her shoulder where the pair had run off to. "They took my reticule! Aren't you going after them?"

He laughed again. "No."

"No?"

"As in, decidedly not." He crossed his arms over his chest and glared at her.

Arabella had never heard such a thing. "Well, that tells me one very important thing about you, sir."

"Which is?"

"You are no gentleman!"

He laughed again. "I had rather thought you'd come to that conclusion the other night."

She had indeed. But she supposed today she'd been lulled into a false sense of security by his well-cut coat and fine carriage. "You truly intend to just sit there and ignore a lady's plight?"

He snorted. "A lady's plight! I will point out that you wouldn't be in such a 'plight' if you had listened to me in the first place. Nor have we settled the matter of whether or not you are a lady."

Arabella had the suspicion he was right—about the

first part— but she certainly wasn't ready to concede that point—or any other—just yet. Instead, she swiped her now gloveless hands over her skirt. "I would have been perfectly safe, save for a bit of uncommonly bad luck."

"Uncommon, my aunt Abigail," he barked with laughter.

"Sir, I will point out that this is Mayfair," she told him, adding a stubborn tromp of her boot, as if planting herself in hallowed ground.

"This is London, you silly goose. Do you think the residents of Seven Dials find the air too rarefied here in Mayfair for their tastes?"

Seven Dials! She glanced around. Why, they wouldn't dare!

Yet . . . as she looked about this time, she saw the streets in an entirely new light. And when a pair of sharp-eyed looking men stepped out of the alleyway, she didn't hesitate to scramble up into the seat beside her own ruffian.

The devil she knew, as it were.

Before he had a chance to laugh at her again, Arabella sat up, smoothing out her skirts, and then paused, her bare hands held out before her. "Oh, no!"

"What is it?" he said, picking up the reins and moving the curricle into the flow of traffic.

She turned her hand this way and that. "That little imp not only managed to take my gloves, but my ring as well."

"Was the ring of value?"

Arabella paused, looking down at the white telltale reminder of where it had been, the indentation where it had sat so coldly and heavily for the past few years.

"Not much," she conceded. "My aunt gave it to me when I—"

She very nearly said "made my presentation at court," but stopped herself. For then he would know she wasn't just some *cit*'s daughter.

As it was he was looking at her, his dark brows cocked up like raven's wings, suspicious and searching for any bit of information.

"My birthday. Last year. Rather ugly, actually," she finished. The latter part was true. It had been an ugly stone in an even uglier setting, but she'd worn it because it was about the only gift she'd ever received from her mother's side of the family.

A mother she'd never known. And her mother's sister only in passing.

Arabella knew why— her mother's family blamed her, and in turn her father, for her mother's death.

If not for her birth, her mother's life would not have been lost.

Such was the guilt and burden that had lain upon her since she'd heard the first whisperings of the servants as to why there was a duke, but no duchess.

Her aunt, on the other hand, had never concealed her feelings for her niece, looking upon Arabella as a poor recompense for the loss of a beloved sister.

And no matter how many times Papa had told her that her mother's passing hadn't been her fault, the ring had been a daily reminder that the rest of the world thought otherwise.

"Yes, well, with it gone, I needn't worry about losing it," she told him.

Because indeed, her hand and her heart did feel lighter without it.

Chapter 4

"So I have saved you from a reckoning," her rescuer observed as he picked up the reins and began to drive again.

"Yes, I suppose so." It nearly did Arabella in to admit as much.

"Then you owe me a boon."

Her head swiveled. "A what?"

"A boon. A favor." He waggled his brows at her, his eyes filled with mirth. It gave him a boyish charm that he didn't deserve. For it made him altogether irresistible.

Arabella looked away. "I know what a boon is, but I hardly see how you've earned one." Truly, he was as insufferable as he was handsome.

"I saved you from certain doom," he pointed out as they drove past the now disappointed pair of sharps.

"You didn't save my reticule," she pointed out.

"I told you to stay put," he reminded her.

"I would think as a gentleman—which you claim to be—that such an act would be done without expecting a favor in return."

"I *am* a gentleman—" he insisted.

"If you say," she muttered under her breath, still smarting from his earlier comment about her own standing as a lady.

As it was, the rogue ignored her. "Gentleman or not, I think I am due a boon. Rescuing you from the street could very well have put me in harm's way."

"You did nothing more than sit in this carriage and laugh at my misfortune," she pointed out.

"Be that as it may, I was here if you truly needed me. And I might point out, you insisted you could take care of yourself."

It was rather humiliating to realize how little she knew of being on her own. She glanced around the streets before her and knew that navigating them without protection might not be the best choice.

She needed an escort. A guide. A rogue. Looking again at the man beside her, her gaze narrowed. "What sort of favor?"

"Say we finish what we nearly started the other night at the ball."

Arabella stilled. Certainly he wasn't suggesting . . .

Then again, this was the same man who'd traced his fingers over her with a practiced air and proposed that she . . .

Well, never mind what he'd proposed. *That* wasn't going to happen.

But she knew this: she needed him. Not that she wanted to admit as much. So she feigned an air of indifference. "You said a great many things that night. I barely remember—"

"Liar. The blush on your cheeks says otherwise."

She pursed her lips together. Did he have to sound so confident? So sure of himself? Never mind that he was right.

Actually, every night since the ball, she'd lain in the quiet of her lonely room and tallied up everything he'd suggested, how he'd touched her, where he'd stroked her, one by one, like one might count a string of pearls.

I'll trace my tongue over you, again and again . . . I'll fill you . . . stroke you . . . I'll tease you until you come quaking beneath me. . .

She did her best to cool the heat rising on her cheeks and when she glanced over at him she came to a shocking realization. "Now? In the middle of the day? Why, that is impossible."

"Shows you how much you know," he teased.

Oh, she knew. She was forever walking in on Papa and Elinor in some passionate embrace in the library or the hallway as if they were the only two people in the world.

Late at night, in the shadows of the halls. And in the middle of the day. As if the secret world they shared was indiscernible to anyone but them.

A world she knew nothing about, and yet the man beside her did.

Tonight, my sweet, I'll fill you, leave you gasping. . .

He couldn't expect such a boon, could he?

When Arabella slanted a glance at this fellow, what with his dark eyes and thick brown hair, all she could imagine was him finishing what he'd been about to do that night—kiss her; no, make that devour her.

The very thought left her mouth dry, sent her very Tremont blood on its own wild course.

Heavens, if her stuffy, all-too-proper father was willing to have scandalous preludes in the middle of the day . . . what would a rake like this want to do?

"Do stop looking at me as if I mean to ruin you here on

Oxford Street in front of everyone," he said. "That isn't what I meant."

"It isn't?" she asked, hoping she didn't sound as disappointed as she suddenly felt. No matter how much her curiosity tugged at her to discover just why a kiss could turn a perfectly sane person into a madcap fool.

But there was something else to consider. If she truly wanted this day, her own London holiday, she needed help.

His help.

Even as a wild, misguided plan slowly formed in her thoughts, Arabella began to speak. "I will grant you your boon—"

"You'll wha-a-a-t—?"

Apparently not the answer he'd been expecting. "If—" she began.

"If?"

"Yes, if you help me with a rather complicated matter."

"Haven't I already accomplished that?"

"Yes, but I wouldn't be in the straits I am in, if the other night you hadn't—"

"Yes, yes, we've already established my fault in all that—"

"And because I have come to realize that I may not be as prepared as I thought—"

"Unprepared? You? Truly?"

Her nose poked a bit higher, prodded by his teasing. "Yes," she conceded. "It might be true that I don't know London as well as I ought—"

This time he didn't tease. He snorted. "Might?"

"Are you going to argue with me on every point or hear the terms of my agreement?"

He chuckled a bit. "Aha! Your father isn't a *cit*, he's a lawyer."

She sniffed with disdain and imagined the second black eye her father would give him for such an insult. "He's no such thing. Why would you say that?"

"Oh, no reason." He chuckled. "Your terms, my fair milk-maid?"

"I have two—no, make that three things I would like to do today. And if you are willing to escort me, then I will grant you a . . . a . . ." Oh, bother she couldn't say it.

For in her mind's eye, her imagination ran wild. At least until she squared her shoulders and did her utmost to set aside such scandalous thoughts.

Oh, bother, if she was going to take charge of her day, then she'd demmed well better be upfront about it.

"Your boon," she forced out. When his eyes lit up with that same lascivious light that had lured her outside last night, she hastily added, "But only a kiss."

Wasn't it as Papa always said? The devil is in the details.

One kiss and only one kiss.

Yes, that would be sufficient.

Wouldn't it?

"Three things you would like to do," he began, adjusting the ribbons in his hands. "Sounds rather mythical."

"I don't need a hero," she told him. "Just an escort."

"Good to know," he told her. "My days of heroism are well behind me."

Kingsley glanced over at the gamine bit of muslin next to him and knew there was one thing he certainly couldn't do.

Let her go.

And not because he wanted her or her kiss.

Not in the least.

Oh, she was fetching enough—those wide blue eyes, that fair skin, and worse, because he'd held her, he knew exactly the lines and curves beneath her gown. What held him back was a liveliness to her that seemed to bubble just beneath the surface, as if being held back by a low flame.

It sparked in her eyes, it teased at her lips when she smiled. And he had a feeling that when she laughed, when something truly amused her, it had that infectious sort of quality that made everyone else around her smile, want to share in her mischief.

So yes, she intrigued him. But that was all she could be.

An intriguing bit of muslin.

More to the point, he could hardly let this chit loose in London. She'd end up being robbed of everything right down to her boots, or worse, end up in some Seven Dials whorehouse.

Beside him, she was muttering again. "Oh, bother!"

"What is it?"

"You're traveling somewhere," she said, nodding over her shoulder at the valise and trunk strapped to the back of his curricle. "And here I thought you were free for the day."

"Yes, well—" he began, looking at the reminders of what was ahead of him.

Kingsley did his best not to shudder—for if he was being honest, he was in the same sort of scrape she was. He didn't want to go home.

He'd been avoiding this trip for days, but when yesterday's summons had arrived, borne in hand by his father's long-suffering secretary—complete with a secondhand lecture on familial duties long-neglected—he'd had no choice but to pack up his bags and turn his carriage toward Sussex.

That, and he was broke. His inheritance from his grandfather was gone. He'd managed to live on it all these years—avoiding any indebtedness to his father—though it hadn't been a fortune to begin with, and with it spent, so was his freedom.

At least the bruise around his eye was now fading, so his mother wouldn't fuss over his less-than-perfect appearance and give his father more evidence of his "unruly state."

"I would never have asked, if I'd—" she told him, making a small sigh as she looked back at the valise.

"Yes, well, it isn't all that important—" Kingsley took another look at the trunk. After all, how long could her three tasks take? The errands of an innocent miss? Most likely he'd find himself having to endure traipsing past the animals at the Tower. Or perhaps a show at Astley's Circus. Most likely, some shopping on Bond Street. Ices at Gunter's.

He'd be done by teatime and whatever pique had set her off to abandon her home and family would be abated by then so he could set her down at her doorstep and still make it home to the Abbey before supper was finished.

His mother did like to make a long-winded production of the evening meal.

Certainly if he arrived in the afternoon as he'd planned, that would only give his parents additional hours to go on and on about the paragon they'd chosen for him to marry.

Or he could trim away some of that needless nagging and spend the day with this troublesome minx.

And if he were willing to admit it, he rather liked the idea of spending the day with her.

"I suppose I could help you," he offered slowly. Immediately her face brightened, that impetuous smile on her lips enticing him to consider that perhaps a day wouldn't be enough. "Yet there is one problem—"

"There is?"

"I don't know your name."

She stilled immediately, her smile shifting as she bit her lips shut. Even her bright eyes narrowed in alarm.

"Your name? You have one, don't you?" he teased.

This was enough to goad her into giving up some hint of who she might be. "Birdie. My family calls me Birdie."

He supposed a nickname was better than nothing. "Birdie, then. Nice to meet you."

She nodded, then she looked at him.

Oh, yes, he needed to give up something as well. A name. At least one of his. He certainly wasn't going to give her his real name. She could turn out to be yet another pretty face looking to raise her standing in society with an advantageous marriage. He'd been all but mobbed when he'd first come to Town years ago.

And that had been one of the myriad of reasons why he'd joined up once he'd discovered just what lengths a miss might go to gain a lofty title. At the time, the French had seemed an easier adversary.

So he used the name that had gotten him into the army without detection. The one that had served him all these years. The one his friends found so amusing.

"Kingsley," he told her. His maternal grandfather's name.

For it had been the old codger who had bought him his commission when his father had refused.

"Kingsley," she said, as if trying it out. "Just Kingsley?"

He knew what she was asking. Was he a lordling, an honorable, a sir, or perhaps some sort of heir with an honorific attached to this moniker? Well, if she wasn't going to be forthcoming, neither was he.

"Just Kingsley will do."

"Excellent, Just Kingsley," she teased in return. "Do we have a bargain?"

"Indeed we do," he told her, pulling off one of his driving gloves and sticking out his hand.

She took his great big paw in hers, her bare fingers slipping into his grasp, and he was struck with how her hand fit into his. The trust and innocence that was even now being placed into his grasp.

Into his protection.

"Let's be at it," he told her, letting go of her hand, for suddenly the magnitude of what he was being entrusted with became a bit overwhelming. "Where to first?"

"Where were we?" Arabella asked, smoothing her hands over her skirt. Silently his name ran through her thoughts as she recalled how it had been to have him holding her hand.

Kingsley.

Hardly the name of a desperate rogue, she had to imagine, but then again, she couldn't recall ever having heard it in Society. When she looked up, she found him gazing at her inquisitively. "Oh, yes. My three choices of where I would like to go."

"Seven Dials?" he ventured.

"No, you ninny," she shot back. "I want to go—" She looked around and then spotted a broadsheet identical to the one she'd seen a day or so ago. "I want to go there," she told him firmly, pointing at the sheet flapping in the breeze.

He looked over in that direction and squinted. "You want to go see a shipment of Danish flutes?"

Arabella did a double take, and there indeed above her choice was a listing from a recent ship, but that was hardly what she wanted to do, on this, her last day of freedom. "No, you scalawag, the advertisement below it."

"Scalawag?" He didn't appear affronted. More like amused.

"Yes, most decidedly."

"Did you just come to that conclusion?" he asked.

"No," she hemmed a bit. "My father referred to you as such." She paused for a moment. "Actually, he did so several times over the last week. And having become reacquainted with you, I think he is correct. Scalawag rather fits."

She thought once again of her lost reticule.

"My father would probably agree. He thinks me quite the—"

"Are you changing the subject?"

"Am I?" Apparently he'd thought she wouldn't notice.

"Yes. I want to go there"—she pointed again at the sheet—"and you promised. That is my first choice for the day."

"You can't be serious?" He glanced over at the broadsheet.

Wilson the Irish Bulldog v. Cormack the Giant
Boxing Match of the Century
Crampton Downs

Now it was her turn to raise a lofty pair of brows in challenge.

"You are." He sank in his seat a bit as if he wasn't too sure what to do next. "Might I point out that ladies are not seen in such places? A boxing match, indeed!"

"You asked me where I wanted to go, and I told you. Are you going back on our agreement?"

His jaw worked back and forth and she could tell he didn't like his honor being called into question. "You can't go like that," he said, waving a hand over her.

"What? Without my gloves?"

"No, like a lady," he told her. "You'll stand out. Proper ladies do not go to such places."

"Oh, so now I am proper lady?" She crossed her arms over her chest.

"If you weren't, we'd have settled the matter of my boon a sennight ago."

Yes, well, he had her there.

Nor was he done. "The only women who go to boxing matches are the ones who are . . . are . . ." Now it was his turn to stammer over semantics.

"Are?"

"Available," he finally said.

"Available?"

He waggled his brows at her and leaned over as if he were going to steal a kiss.

Her eyes widened. "Oh, no!" She shoved her elbow into his ribs, sending him back to his side of the carriage. "Truly, I can't go dressed in this gown?"

He shook his head.

"Oh, bother. It is the first stare of fashion, but then I suppose at a boxing match, fashion is hardly of interest."

"No, decidedly not." How much a man could mill his opponent, how much one had wagered on the champ, and who had a ready bottle, yes, those were of interest.

"Then I suppose there is no way around it," she said with a sigh, as she glanced down at her gown.

"No, I'm afraid in that rig you would stand out," he agreed, his smug tone implying she should choose a more sedate adventure.

"Stand out? No, I mustn't do that," she agreed, looking around. "Oh, do stop the carriage—right over there." She pointed at the nearby corner. And once again, he barely had the horses paused before she jumped down. "Don't go anywhere. I'll be right back."

Kingsley shook his head. What sort of trouble was she up to now?

Then he took a good look at the establishment she'd rushed to enter and he had one of those moments of premonition that had served him so well all those years in Spain.

That sense that disaster was right at hand.

She wouldn't, he told himself. *No, she wouldn't dare...*

Then he remembered, she hadn't any money—her reticule had been taken, as had her ring. He sat back in his seat and smiled, feeling both relief and a bit of triumph.

Penniless, there was little she could do in such a shop. She'd be exiting any moment.

At least he kept telling himself that as he waited . . . and waited . . . and waited.

Then just when he was about to climb down and go inside to see what trouble she'd gotten herself mired into this time, a stunning creature in a red-trimmed gown stepped out the door.

If the red color wasn't enough to catch the eye, it was the lady herself who left him breathless—a red and paisley hat with a wide lacy brim that left him unable to make out her features, but he could see her full lips set in a wry smile. And why shouldn't this magnificent creature be smiling—for she very well knew how her gown dipped low to reveal a full bosom. One that teased a man to take a second glance.

Then this unlikely Paragon stopped before him. "Well, Kingsley, are you going to help me up?"

He blinked. Then he stared. Then he just gaped in shock.

Good God! She hadn't?

Oh, but she had.

"Birdie?"

"Well, who else would I be, you goose? Now be a gentleman, come down and help me up. This gown wasn't made for dashing about."

No, it was made for catching a man's eye. Inviting him to let his gaze linger and his thoughts consider what it would be like to remove it.

"How did you . . . I mean, you hadn't any . . . Good God, Birdie! What did you do?"

He scrambled down and came around the carriage, glancing around to see if anyone else had seen her. Then he handed her up and got back in his seat even as she was tucking a bundle beneath the seat. "Whatever are you wearing?"

"You said my gown wasn't proper for a boxing match, so I acquired one that is. This will do, won't it? I look quite the Cyprian." She tipped her head just so, and smiled so her lips rose only slightly, a knowing sort of glance that no innocent miss should have mastered.

"How . . . How?" he managed.

"My pearl ear bobs," she confided, one hand rising to her now bare earlobe. "I traded them." She shrugged at their loss, but then adjusted her grand hat and smiled anew. "I've never worn red before."

"You should," he said without thinking, immediately regretting the hasty confession for it only managed to encourage her.

"I should?" she asked, preening a bit.

"Assuredly," he muttered.

"False compliments will not gain you any additional boons," she informed him, once again the proper miss.

"Believe me, in that gown you will be fending off compliments of all sorts. And believe me, they will all be seeking boons."

A s they left the cobbled streets and close-knit houses of London, Kingsley's companion brightened noticeably. She tipped her hat back to let the sun fall on her face—having no missish reserve about a chance of freckles. When all that could heard was the clip-clop of the horses' hooves, and larks and robins singing in the hedges, she leaned back and grinned, as content as a cat in the creamery.

But not so content as to remain silent.

"What sort of heroisms did you perpetuate?"

The question came out of nowhere and took Kingsley aback. "Excuse me?"

"You said earlier your days of heroism were behind you."

He glanced over at her. "I did, didn't I?" Then he went back to driving.

And for a while, they ambled along in silence, the road continuing to give way to the green English countryside.

"Care to elaborate?" she prodded.

Kingsley turned to her. "Care to tell me where you live?"

Her lips pursed together. But not for long. "We cannot drive along in complete silence."

"Whyever not?"

Birdie heaved a sigh. "If one is to be considered good company, they should provide some sort of conversation."

"Excellent," he agreed. "Shall we discuss who your father is? Or perhaps, where we might find him?"

Her brow furrowed into a dark line. Apparently not a subject she approved of. So he tried again.

"What? Don't those subjects meet with your approval?"

She shot him a hot, scathing glance.

Kingsley shrugged. "Very well then. What finishing school in Bath did you attend?"

"However did you know—" she admitted, before she realized what she had just said.

"Aha!" he barked in triumph. "You went to finishing school, Miss Birdie. Three years of curtsying and—"

"I only went for a year," she huffed.

"A year? What happened?" He grinned at her. "Landed in the suds, did we?"

"I don't care to discuss the matter."

"I would. Whatever did you do?" Now he was the one who not only warmed to the subject but brightened.

"Perhaps you were right before. Silence *is* a better companion."

"Hardly. Not when you have such a secret."

She glanced away, as if the passing scenery had taken a delightful and engaging turn.

"You argued with the mistress," he ventured.

She waved him off, as if such a thing was trifling and far beneath her.

"You got caught trying to sneak out," he proposed.

She sniffed. "I never got caught."

"Never?"

Again, the only answer he received was a scathing glance.

"Now, whyever would a young lady sneak out of her proper school? I can't think of a single reason," he posed, tugging at his chin as if the answer, any answer, eluded him.

"Excellent," she replied. "Then shall we discuss your heroics?"

Kingsley snorted. "Not until you tell me who it was you were sneaking out to meet."

Her mouth fell open and just as quickly snapped shut. But the most telling evidence was the deep blush that rose up on her cheeks.

They were coming around a sharp bend in the road and as they turned, the infamous view of Sir Hubert's grand mansion rose before them like the Taj Mahal.

"The horror of that monstrosity never ceases to amaze

me," Birdie declared, making a point of looking in the opposite direction.

Kingsley had the sense that she was testing him, for in some circles Sir Hubert's house was considered a masterpiece of luxury. The knighted merchant, who'd made his fortune in India and returned to England wealthy beyond imagination and completely lacking in taste, was fond of saying about his homage to every architectural style from the Nile to Peking, from the Greeks to the current Romantic mania, "It is the finest erection to be found."

"He had the right notion with the columns," Kingsley told her. "At least with the first four."

Her brow furrowed as she looked back at the house and then at him. As she realized exactly what he was saying, she grinned. "It's unfortunate he didn't stop at the fourth. For they are the finest columns to be found."

They laughed together and quickly launched into a discussion of all that was wrong with Sir Hubert's hubris and architecture and art, and the miles fell away as Kingsley related some of the fantastic and wild structures he had seen in his travels. Paris. The Alps. Venice. Rome.

"I would love to see the sun rise over the mountains, like you described," Birdie said, a wistful note to her words.

"Don't think to add that to your list," he teased. Yet despite his own warning, his imagination conjured up an image of her standing there atop a ridge, smiling coyly over her shoulder as the first rays of morning light burst over the ragged horizon. Kingsley tamped such a tempting vision down. "We haven't time today."

"No, I suppose not," she agreed, slanting an equally wistful glance up at him as if she had been pondering just that notion.

Take her to the Alps, indeed. "Not even to Paris," he added.

And that time it was more for himself.

CHAPTER 5

As they pulled into the field where the boxing match was to be held, Arabella rose up in her seat and surveyed the grand sight before her, images of Paris and the Alps fading from her thoughts.

For here it was, her first adventure. And such a sight it was.

The wide downs were filled with carriages and men, along with an array of canopies that had been thrown up here and there. It was like a large country fair, and her heart hammered with excitement.

And something else. She couldn't help glancing over her shoulder at the road that had brought them here—the one that led back to London. Where her family was most likely sick with worry over her disappearance. She bit her lips together and suppressed a sharp feeling of guilt.

Then again, how many times had Great-Aunt Josephine disappeared on her own and everyone always assumed she'd find her way home. Had for decades.

Yes, that was it, she told herself. She was merely following in her scandalous relation's footsteps.

Still, looking around the vast crowds, Arabella felt a frisson of something else.

A shiver of fear.

She'd never been anywhere where she wasn't surrounded by family or servants or close friends. And now all she had with her was this man. This stranger. This Kingsley.

She supposed this would be nothing to her independent milkmaid, but to her—the daughter of a duke, sheltered and kept well away from anything that could be called common—well, Arabella suspected she might be in over her head.

Oh, not in the same way she'd been at the bakeshop, but . . .

"I cannot wait to see Wilson's uppercut," she told Kingsley, tamping aside her fears and regrets. "It is said he learned it from Dutch Sam. Well, he experienced it at the hands of Dutch Sam. That wily fellow planted a most excellent facer on Wilson last year that left him down after forty-seven rounds."

"Truly?" Kingsley remarked absently, for he was, as she had been, surveying the scene, and from the way his brow was drawn together, it was obvious he was not as pleased by the sight before them as she was.

"No, I won't," he said, adjusting the reins in his grasp. "I cannot."

She caught hold of his sleeve. "Whatever do you mean, 'I cannot'? Why, I hardly think a single afternoon of boxing will be my undoing—" Then she glanced down at her own hand atop his sleeve and pulled it back.

"It isn't the match," he told her sharply, "but the company." He waved his hand out over the crowd before them

"What? A bunch of London toffs?" Arabella sniffed.

"Those toffs are going to take one look at you and decide

you are a much more interesting sight than the one in the ring."

"Bah!" she scoffed. "In your company, no one will dare bother me." She nodded toward an opening in the line of waiting carriages.

He still didn't look convinced.

"I will do whatever you ask, Kingsley," she told him. Pleaded, really. Oh, to be so close to an actual boxing match and not be able to see it—well, that was worse than just having to content herself with reading about the matches in *The Sporting Magazine*.

"Whatever I say?" he asked.

"Oh, yes!" she promised. "I will be a paragon of obedience."

Again he snorted, but he did move the carriage off the road and handed the reins to one of the local lads who came to the matches just to manage the horses and make a few extra coins. After flipping the lad a bob, Kingsley climbed down and caught hold of her, swinging her free from the carriage.

Arabella landed against him—her feet tangling in her elaborate hem—and she had to catch hold of his jacket until she could find her footing.

It was a dangerous place to find herself. Back in his arms, her hands splayed across his chest.

She could feel his heart, beating soundly beneath her palm. Strong and sure.

His heat, a whiff of bay soap, leather, and horses, and all the things that made a man so very different from a woman surrounded her. Left her feeling far more vulnerable than she ever had.

She was trusting this man with . . . well, with everything. Her reputation. Her safety.

Her heart.

Her breath stopped in her chest. Where had that thought come from?

She didn't dare look up at him. Get lost in those eyes of his—the way they seemed to smoke with desire. With tempting lights from faraway places meant to lure her onto paths into the unknown.

His arm curved around her hip as he steadied her, his other hand playfully batting at the ridiculous collection of plumes atop her bonnet. She wanted to lean in so their bodies were nearly joined. She wanted . . .

Oh, goodness, she didn't know what she wanted.

All this was so intimate and playful, as if they were meant to be thus—together. Together traveling about the Continent. Exploring Paris. Pottering about Rome.

Just them. Just the two of them where no one could dictate their future, their days, their hearts.

But that was impossible and best not dwelt upon, Arabella realized.

Instead, with a determined air, she stepped back and away from him. Shook out her skirt and straightened her bonnet, all the while willing her heart to stop pounding in such a haphazard fashion.

"Whatever could go wrong?" she managed, her mouth dry and the fateful words nearly choking her, even as she finally got the nerve to look up at him, caught instantly in the heat of his gaze.

Trapped. Bound. Yes, that was it. *Bound.*

For she felt as if there was an invisible thread between them, weaving them closer, pulling with it desires unknown.

As she shivered, she changed her mind. No, make it a chain. A heavy, unbreakable binding.

A thread she could snap. But this . . .

This heat, this promise, it would not go unanswered for long. For here he was, stepping closer to her, his head tipping down as if he was about to kiss her, his hand reaching for hers . . .

Not that they had much time to discover what could come next, for Kingsley's arrival hadn't gone unnoticed.

"Ho there!" called out a voice. "Kingsley! Is that truly you?"

Arabella felt, rather than saw, Kingsley flinch.

"Or should I say Major Kingsley?" came the query.

Major? she mouthed at him.

"Not a word out of you," he told her. More like warned her. More to the point, he stepped back from her, putting a bit of distance between them, so that whatever had bound them together moments earlier snapped.

"Not a word," he repeated.

Arabella shivered. There was so much she didn't know about him. "But—"

Kingsley's dark brow furrowed into a hard line. "Speak a word and we go back to London."

She pressed her lips together and nodded.

Kingsley, make that Major Kingsley, turned around. "Rollins? You devil, whatever are you doing here?"

"Rare luck," Rollins declared, extending a hand and taking Kingsley's in a furious and exuberant shake. "Not often I come up to London, but had a need to see my man of business and a certain lady—" the fellow said with a laugh, until his glance lit on Arabella. Then, if it was possible, the newcomer's smile widened, his eyes glowing with mischief. "What have we here, Kingsley?"

Kingsley glanced over his shoulder at Arabella. "An acquaintance of mine."

"Acquaintance, indeed. She's a Diamond, you devil. Madame, I am Rollins," he said pushing Kingsley aside and taking up Arabella's hand, bringing her fingers to his eager lips. "Whoever might you be?"

She was about to open her mouth, but Kingsley stopped that.

"Don't bother, my good man. Doesn't speak a bit of English."

Rollins drew back at this news. "Doesn't—"

"Not a word," Kingsley lied convincingly, adding a woeful shake of his head that would have served him well on the stage.

"You are a rare one," Rollins laughed. "Most fellows who were at Waterloo brought back French sabers or some gaudy piece of art they claim is a Rubens, but not you." Again Rollins whistled. "You bring back a French masterpiece." He turned to her. "Excuse my confusion before. Oh, mademoiselle—" he began, launching into a long-winded speech in schoolboy French which he obviously hadn't used since his university days, given the way he mangled his pronunciation.

Again Arabella went to open her mouth, for she did speak fluent French, but Kingsley was too quick for her.

"Stop torturing that poor tongue of yours," he told Rollins. "She doesn't speak French either."

Now both Rollins and Arabella shot him puzzled glances.

"This is Klara, and she's Flemish. You don't speak Flemish, do you?" Kingsley asked his friend, taking Arabella's fingers out of the man's grasp and winding her hand around his forearm.

"Not a demmed word," the man admitted. "Still, she must have learned a few—"

Kingsley shook his head, but his eyes were all merriment, as if he was letting his friend in on the latest *on dit*. "Happily, she hasn't a bit of wit to her. Finds English utterly baffling."

Oh, the wretched devil! Arabella's eyes flew open and her mouth was about to as well, but Kingsley's brows arched ever so slightly at her.

Do as I say, he silently reminded her.

Arabella had a thousand retorts just blistering her tongue, but the lure of the boxing match held her from unleashing them. That, and her estimation of this man continued to shift.

Major Kingsley.

He'd fought at Waterloo.

This rogue wouldn't be able to put off a discussion on heroics now that she had the truth of it. Well, a piece. A hint.

She slanted another glance at him, holding back a peppering of questions, for he had caught hold of her hand and folded it into the crook of his arm.

"Surprised to see you here," Rollins began as the three of them started across the downs. He spoke over Arabella's head as if she was the witless and English-challenged piece Kingsley claimed her to be. "Had heard you were to be married."

If being called witless wasn't enough, this was news of another sort. It was all she could do not to swivel her gaze up to his and then demand answers.

Kingsley was to be married? Was that where he had been going when she'd bumped into him earlier?

To his wedding?

She and Rollins both looked to him for answers.

"Country gossip," Kingsley told Rollins in a lofty, off-handed manner.

"Good news that," his friend declared. "Would be sad to see you have to set up your nursery so soon after returning. Though did expect you back sooner."

"I stayed for the peace talks then did a bit of poking about. France, the Alps, Rome."

"Old ruins, I imagine," Rollins said with a laugh. "Fusty art. Hiking with the natives. You've always been an odd one."

To Arabella it hadn't sounded odd—no, it had sounded heavenly.

"Also heard you were shot," Rollins remarked.

"I was."

Arabella nearly tripped, but Kingsley held her steady. He'd been shot? Where? When?

That he'd recovered was obvious, but Arabella's heart clenched at the thought of him being struck by a bullet.

Yet the finality behind his brief answer made it clear it wasn't a subject that Kingsley was going to explain, and Rollins was enough of a gentleman not to ask.

But that didn't stop a whirlwind of questions from turning inside Arabella.

So Kingsley was Major Kingsley . . . which meant he was a gentleman.

He'd fought at Waterloo. Been wounded. And now was slated to be married.

And given the flinch that had rippled through him like a slice from a saber, she had to imagine it wasn't a union of his choosing.

Whoever was he supposed to be marrying?

Hardly anyone of substance since she hadn't heard of him or any prattle of a match to him.

Her mouth pressed together. What a vexing puzzle.

But no more vexing than this Rollins, who persisted in their company. For as long as he remained beside them, Arabella was forced to hold her tongue.

"So she's Flemish, you say," Rollins remarked, examining Arabella again like one might a racing filly.

If he put his hand on her withers, or anywhere else, she was going to demonstrate exactly what she knew of an uppercut.

"Yes, Flemish," Kingsley said, winking at her as if it were the grandest joke he'd ever heard.

Oh, he could grin and flirt all he wanted, but she was going to pay him back for all this.

With interest.

Even if she had promised to follow his lead.

Though she certainly hadn't promised to be a witless Flemish prostitute.

"Probably much cheaper than some French bird," Rollins noted.

Well, she couldn't stop her cheeks from flaming, but she could tip her hat so the wide brim hid the telltale scarlet of her embarrassment.

Oh, of all the humiliations to suffer. Now she was to be a bargain piece as well?

"That is yet to be seen," Kingsley said over her enormous bonnet, once again swatting at the plumes, and both men laughed.

Arabella did not. After all, she didn't speak English. Besides that, she was fuming so hotly, she wondered if she could have gotten out a coherent sentence as it was.

But then she had her revenge. "Must go place my bet on Cormack," Rollins said, as if suddenly remembering why he was here. "Have it on good authority that is where the winning purse will fall."

Rollins gave her one more look, then did the unbelievable; he slapped her on her backside, and grinned at her. "You are a most excellent piece, Klara" he said, loudly, as if his added volume would make it intelligible to her. "Flemish!" the man declared to no one in particular with a delighted bit of wonder. "Who knew?" Then Rollins laughed again and hurried toward one of the tables where bets were being tallied.

Kingsley doubled over. Not with just a friendly chuckle, but a deep, rolling bark of a laugh that rumbled out of him in delighted triumph.

Meanwhile, Arabella rubbed her stinging backside. "Was that necessary?" she demanded now that Rollins was well out of earshot.

"I thought so," Kingsley told her between guffaws.

"Truly?" Arabella struck a puffed-up pose and did her best imitation of him. "She doesn't speak a word of English."

"I thought it quite inspired."

"You would." She huffed a bit. "And if anyone is witless, it is your friend. Cormack, indeed! Anyone with a lick of sense knows Wilson has more stamina. Your Rollins is going to lose his shirt."

"Should we go save him from his folly?"

"Not in the least. Vulgar man!"

"I warned you." Kingsley took up her hand again. "A boxing match is not a place for a lady. You are a lady, are you not, Lady—" He left the last part open for her to provide the answer.

"I'm sorry, I don't speak English," she reminded him. "Were you saying something?"

He laughed again and as they continued to stroll through the crowd, Arabella quickly realized that Kingsley, no, make that Major Kingsley, had been right about one thing. There weren't very many women about.

And the ones who were there were, as he'd claimed, hardly proper.

A blowzy lady in a bright yellow gown strolled by with a tall rake at her side, his arm curled most improperly around her waist.

But it was the look in the man's eyes that stopped Arabella, for she'd never seen a man look at a woman quite like that.

Intimately. Longingly. Wickedly.

He looked at the lady as if he knew all her delights and couldn't wait to discover them once again.

And the woman? She laughed without a care in the world. Brightly and happily.

Arabella wondered if this demoiselle could whistle. Of course she could. She supposed such a woman could whistle and do a whole lot more, given her companion's admiring gaze.

What would it be like to hold a man's attention thusly? As if he wanted to do nothing more than devour you?

"Am I to remain silent the entire day?" she asked.

"That depends," Kingsley said, leading them to a good vantage point.

"On what?"

"How much Flemish you know."

She glanced over her shoulder at the woman, and considered that perhaps speech was highly overrated.

She leaned closer until her hip rested against Kingsley's, and then hitched herself right up against him, both hands curling possessively around his arm. "How is this? Flemish enough for you?"

Kingsley didn't know if he'd ever seen anything more amusing than Birdie's outraged expression when he'd introduced her to Rollins.

Flemish! What a fine joke.

Until now.

For here she was, curled into his side, her fingers wound onto his forearm, her hip nestled up against him. He could even feel her breast pressed to him.

And she fit. Perfectly to his side. As she had in his arms the night of the ball.

Flirt like a coquette, will she? He'd show her the consequences by pulling her right into his arms and kissing her senseless—right here, right now.

Oh, that would put an end to her charade.

But he didn't dare. He'd nearly kissed her by the carriage—holding her up against him. And if he had . . . Well, perhaps Rollins's arrival had been a bit of luck.

Or misfortune.

Kissing Birdie would be a disaster. For it would lead to something far more tempting, something that would take time he could ill afford.

Unfortunately, he must keep reminding himself of the necessity of being at the Abbey no later than . . . tomorrow.

Never mind that he had vowed to be there this very afternoon. Well, a few more hours wouldn't be the end of his parent's scheme.

But in the meantime . . .

He glanced around and spied a man selling food nearby. "Are you hungry?" he asked, recalling her lost purchase at the bakeshop.

She paused and then grinned. "Famished."

They strolled over to the booth and he bought them both sausage rolls and they ate in happy companionship, the sort of life Kingsley had always longed for. Loved, when he'd dropped being someone else's son and taken his grandfather's name.

And at some point—he truly didn't know when—he'd become Kingsley.

Just Kingsley, as he'd told her. Oh, how he'd reveled in the freedom of it.

"Would you ever go back?" she was asking, a bit of grease rolling down her chin.

He reached over and wiped it clean with his thumb. "Back?"

"To all the places you've visited?"

The names ran through his thoughts. Paris . . . Rome . . . Venice.

The memories were like the stars in her eyes. Now too far away to grasp.

"I don't know."

"I suppose you needn't go," she remarked, finishing the last bite and heaving a contented sigh. "You've seen it all."

Kingsley laughed. "No one could do that. Not even in a lifetime."

"You could try," she suggested, her chin tipping upward, a defiant tilt that said she'd surely give her best effort, or an offer.

I'd help.

Help was not what he needed. "I must see to my obligations," he said, more to himself than her.

"Bother them," she declared. But he suspected she was speaking of her own encumbrances.

"Yes, indeed," he agreed. "At least for today."

She smiled in agreement and he did his best to ignore the curve of her sweet lips.

This is what came of spending three years on his own.

Blessedly, simply alone, he reminded himself.

When Waterloo had been won, the blood and mud all washed away, he'd longed only to see beauty.

To put the horrific images of that battle well behind him. To hear only the songs of birds, the lowing of cattle, the beat of hooves, anything but the anguished cries of the dying.

He'd sold out his commission as soon as he could, and taken his horse and ridden east from Paris.

No valet, no batman. None of the trappings a man of his birth and rank could summon.

And it had never occurred to him that he'd done all this because he could. At least not until today.

Even earlier when she'd complained of her lack of freedom, he'd been rather dismissive.

Conditioned to think that young ladies belonged only in London drawing rooms.

A fate he wouldn't have consigned on the lowliest of ensigns.

Yet he could see now this slip of muslin never would have such freedom. Not as a miss, nor as a wife.

Not unless she became a widow before her dotage, and even then she'd be trailed about by some fawning hired companion, a maid, a footman, a driver, and all the other accouterments that came with encumbered travels.

She wouldn't see the sun rise over the Alps. The catacombs beneath Rome. Walk barefoot on an empty beach where it was rumored Aphrodite had once frolicked.

He had done all that, free to make his own choices. A state he thought he preferred until now. And no, it wasn't the moment when she'd curled into him like a cloying little kitten that he'd realized that, but when Rollins had teased him for his travels.

He hadn't mistaken the light in her eyes when he'd described the gondolas in Venice.

Birdie, who had never learned to whistle, also longed to fly.

He might have shown her all that. If they had met before.

The magnitude of Notre Dame. The canals in Venice. The mysteries of Rome. The breathtaking mountains to be climbed in the Alps.

He'd have unfettered her wings and taken her to new heights.

But it was too late. He could no more whisk her off to the Continent than she could fly. By tomorrow, at the very latest, he had to be on his way home.

Today, though, today he'd open her cage as far as he dared.

His as well, he realized when she slanted a sly smile up at him.

The sort that wound around inside him and had him at sixes and sevens. Had him remembering the curves that were rather hard to ignore in that outlandish red gown she was wearing.

"What if—" he began, even as a cheer rose up from the crowd ahead and she tugged at his arm, bringing him back to solid ground.

"Come along or we won't find a good spot for the match," she urged.

Kingsley nodded and left his woolgathering behind as they made their way through the crush. Then he led her to a small rise where she could see over the crowds. "Will this do?"

"Oh, most excellent." Birdie rose up on her toes, her bright blue eyes all sparkle.

He could feel her quivering with excitement, and her joy became his. The shouts, the fervor of the crowd around them, and the sunshine spilling down upon them.

As the first round began, the cheers were deafening, and while Kingsley had been to many a match in his day, there was something about being here with Birdie.

"Use the hook!" she shouted, her hands cupped to her mouth. "HOOK!"

Her small hands fisted and swung at the air. She booed when Cormack made a hard hit and sent her favorite, Wilson, careening over.

When she'd talked of the match, he had taken her interest as more of a rebellious streak than a true passion for sports, but for Birdie boxing was a madness.

Something about her enthusiasm, her eager delight in the sport, told him more about her than her address, name, and lineage ever could have. It was a side of her that would never be seen in a drawing room, or at a ball, or at a formal picnic.

He was looking at the very heart of this woman, and her fire ignited him.

Kingsley shook his head as she called out another set of instructions to the infamous Wilson, and wondered how he was ever going to get her away from this match.

And how he was ever going to let her go.

CHAPTER 6

Arabella had never seen the likes of a real boxing match. Oh, it was far superior to anything she'd ever imagined, especially when an apparently defeated Wilson rose from the turf and pummeled Cormack, tapping the man's claret and sending a shower of blood over the onlookers in front. Arabella couldn't have been more thrilled.

A real, live boxing match. She'd remember this day for the rest of her life.

And she had Kingsley to thank for it. *Major* Kingsley, she reminded herself.

Oh, she could spend all day thusly, and so she would, until, that is, she looked up and spied a familiar face staring at her from across the match.

No, make that gaping at her.

Her breath stopped, for despite her costume, her flamboyant hat, and all her trappings, there was no mistaking the look of shock on the face of Lord Augustus Charles Hustings.

Nor was there any mistaking Lord Augustus, what with

his outlandish choice of a bright purple waistcoat and a jaunty hat that towered over his diminutive height.

Augie! Oh, good heavens, no!

Arabella whirled around and put her back to him, her thoughts racing as to what to do first. Run? Duck into the crowd? Plead a megrim?

"Had enough?" Kingsley teased.

"Um, no. Not in the least," she told him, even as the crowd roared into a cacophony of catcalls and shouts. She couldn't help herself, she turned around only to find Wilson once again down and Cormack crowing about like a cock—really the man was as vain as *The Sporting Magazine* declared—and worse, when she glanced over the crowd again, there was no sign of Augie.

"Where the devil has he gone?" she muttered under her breath. While Arabella was not usually one to use strong language, today of all days was one when she was setting aside everything that was expected of her.

That, and she knew Augie.

He wouldn't give up until he was at her side and had a full accounting.

Trying to appear calm, she searched for her friend and then to her horror spied him pushing his way through the crush.

Oh, bother! He was making a determined beeline for her.

He would. And he'd ruin everything, Augie would. Insist she go home—immediately! Insist she change her clothes. Immediately!

And she hadn't even gotten to the two remaining things on her list.

Now she might not ever.

She whirled around to the major. "Yes, well, that was exciting," she told Kingsley, "but if we are to complete our adventures today, I fear we must get going." She caught his hand and tugged him into the crush.

"So soon?" he asked. "Look! Cormack just took a devil of a hit."

"Yes, yes, that is well and good. I have every confidence in Wilson, but we really must be going," she told him emphatically, knowing full well without even looking that Augie was at their heels.

"Well, if you insist," Kingsley was saying. "This is your day, isn't it?"

"Yes, it is." Or it was until Augie had arrived.

They pressed through the worst of the throng and made their way toward the major's curricle. Arabella was about to sigh with relief that she had escaped detection, when out of the fringe of the crowd came Augie—blocking their path.

Well, as much as a man that small could obstruct anyone.

"Kingsley!" he said in his usual grand style. "Whatever are you doing here with—?"

Arabella panicked and went into a fit of coughing. "Oh, my, excuse me," she choked out between coughs, and in English, forgetting that she was Flemish, and forgetting that she was supposed to be silent.

But the one thing she couldn't do was let Augie finish that sentence.

Whatever are you doing here with Lady Arabella?

She continued to cough and choke, clutching at Kingsley's sleeve. "A drink of something, if you can," she managed, looking up at the man with her best and most practiced flutter of lashes.

This was a moment when the experience of four Seasons came in most handy.

"Aye, Kingsley," Augie echoed. "The lady appears quite parched. Don't you usually keep a flask of wine in your carriage?"

Then it finally struck her. Augie knew him? Oh, this *was* a disaster.

Kingsley glanced over at her and then back at his friend, his face a mix of consternation and dismay. "Yes, I suppose I do. Birdie, do you mind waiting here with an old friend of mine, Lord Augustus Hustings. He's a vagrant and a scoundrel, but he'll keep you safe until I can bring round the carriage."

After a warning glance from Arabella, Augie grinned and told Kingsley, "I would be delighted to be of assistance to your most enchanting and surprising friend."

The major turned to go after the carriage, but not before sending a speculative glance at Arabella. She coughed again for good measure and fluttered her hand at him to hurry along.

Quickly. Before Augie blurted out something telling. Like her real name.

Arabella smiled encouragingly at Kingsley until he was well out of earshot. Then she whirled about on one of her oldest friends. "Augie! What are you doing here?"

He took an affronted step back. "Me? Birdie, what the devil are you doing here? And in *his* company?"

"Whatever is wrong with him?" Her gaze strayed back over her shoulder at Kingsley's retreating figure. "Oh, I grant you he's common enough . . ."

"Common?" Augie sort of choked out.

"Yes, of course," she replied. Truly, sometimes Augie's choices of friends blinded him. Yet in Kingsley's case, she was willing to make an exception. "Though he seems a gentleman of sorts. He was a major after all. I don't suppose they make just anyone a major."

Augie gaped, openmouthed, like a freshly landed trout. "Does your father know about this?" he finally managed to get out, even as he searched his inside coat pockets for a handkerchief, which he used to swab at his damp brow.

Arabella pressed in close and covered his mouth with her hand. "Oh, do be quiet. Of course my father doesn't know about this. My father is dreadful. He's forcing me to wed."

"I know. Marbury's heir."

"Yes, that's the horridly dull fellow." She shuddered and glanced back at Kingsley. Now why couldn't he be the heir to a dukedom?

"That's the—" Augie shook his head as if clearing out an attic's worth of cobwebs. "I do say, Birdie, whyever is that a problem?"

"A problem? I've never even met the man!"

"Never met—" Augie's eyes narrowed. "But Birdie—"

"Oh, please do not 'but Birdie' me!"

"But if you would just let me—"

Arabella had no desire to listen to his admonishments. "Augie, no more. I know my own mind."

He took a step back, his brow furrowed as if he had plenty to say, but to her surprise, managed to agree with her. "Yes, I suppose you do."

Then the man's gaze narrowed and fixed on Kingsley, as if he were laying all the blame on the major's shoulders.

"You know him," Arabella said. "The major, that is."

"Yes." The answer came out in a short clip. "However did you two come to this place?"

She quickly explained how they'd met and what she had asked of the major.

"Asked?" Now it was Augie's turn to laugh. "You most likely demanded his attendance and I'm surprised you didn't ask for the moon as well."

"And why shouldn't I? I've been held like a prisoner all my life." Arabella knew Augie would appreciate a dash of the dramatic. But not today.

"A gilded one, I would point out," he said, his arms folding over his chest as if he thought her better served to be locked back in it.

"You sound like my father."

He ruffled at this, his brow crinkling in outrage. "I'm hardly as stuffy as all that."

"Then don't scold," she advised him. "And you won't tell him that you saw me, will you?"

Augie stepped back, aghast. "Lie to your father?" He shook his head. *Adamantly*. Nor was he done protesting. "He'll skin me alive if he discovers I've aided and abetted all this."

"Not if he doesn't find out," she told him most confidently.

"Your father always finds out," he reminded her. "No, no, I won't hear of this. Birdie, you must go home now or I'll have no choice but to—"

Arabella caught hold of his sleeve. "You tell my father and I'll tell your mother about the redhead you visit in Blooms-bury. Gwen, isn't it? An opera dancer, isn't she?"

His eyes widened in horror. "How the devil do you know—?"

"You were more than squiffy last month at the Bastion ball."

Augie's jaw worked back and forth. For he knew—just as Arabella did—that Lady Prendwick would make her son's life miserable over such a *mésalliance*.

"The consequences of today are all mine," she told him. "Augie, dearest, you are my oldest friend. My best friend. Well, besides your sisters. Please, don't tell my father."

Augie's jaw worked back and forth. "Oh, stuff and bother, Birdie. You will be the death of me."

She clapped her hands together and laughed. "So you will keep my secret?"

He made a tight, short nod. For he was very fond of Gwen.

"And not tell my father? Or Kingsley? It would never do if he knew who I was. He'd take me home in a thrice."

Augie muttered something about "—that, or pack you away to Bedlam," but she ignored him.

She hugged him quickly. "Once I've had my fun, then I shall go home," she promised faithfully, though that didn't stop that now all-too-familiar pang of guilt over the worry her disappearance was most likely causing.

Though weighed against a lifetime married to the dull prospect her father proposed, it seemed a fair trade.

"There is no harm in all this, truly—" she rushed to assure Augie, who appeared to be wavering yet again. "I only want to learn to whistle before I must pay the piper."

"Oh, is that all? If it was whistling you wanted, you need only have asked me," Augie teased. "I can make quite a merry tune." To prove his point, he whistled a naughty ditty.

It was an old joke between them, and Arabella couldn't help herself, she laughed as well.

"Whatever are these three tasks you've charmed Kingsley into doing for you? I won't have you getting him in over his head. Always the Hercules, that one, ready to dash into danger. He's done enough."

The wistful note to Augie's voice gave her pause and she remembered what Rollins had said. "Kingsley was at Waterloo, wasn't he?"

Augie looked up at the major, a light of loyalty and admiration in his eyes. "Yes. And in Spain before that. Acquitted himself quite nobly, though you won't get the story out of him. Heard it from another. Nearly got himself killed—"

Arabella shivered and wrapped her shawl tighter around her shoulders. "Who is he, Augie?"

"Oh, he can't know who you are, but I'm to tell you all his secrets." Her friend laughed.

"No, really, who is he?" she asked, overcome with curiosity.

"That is your task to uncover, my dear girl," he told her. "But you must be kind to the major. Promise me that. And when the time comes, forgiving."

Her gaze wrenched away from the major. "Forgiving? Whyever will I need to forgive him?"

Augie grinned and nodded at a spot just over her shoulder. She turned around to find Kingsley had brought his carriage around, and almost as soon as he stopped he was out and coming around to join them.

"Ho, there. You two forgotten me?" Kingsley asked, his gaze sweeping from one to the other.

"Not in the least," Arabella told him, smiling brightly.

Perhaps a little too brightly, for the major then turned to his friend. "Augie, you devil, don't you get any ideas about the lady. I hope you haven't been filling her ears with lies about me." He looked over at Arabella, his eyes twinkling, merrily. A tempting clarion call that was only for her.

And he must have felt it as well, for he reached out and took her hand. Possessively. His fingers entwined with hers, and instead of ruffling her feathers, leaving her feeling confined, contained, the major's strength lent her a sort of freedom.

With him at her side, she could fly anywhere.

This man could give her the world, her heart's desires.

Her Hercules, as Augie had teased.

"No, he's chiding me to treat you kindly," Arabella told him, doing her best to ignore the new raft of shivers running down her spine.

"Are you ready to go?" he asked.

Arabella nodded, as it hit her. Two more tasks and then he would set her down in front of her father's residence and her freedom would be lost.

Kingsley would be lost.

She slanted a glance up at him from beneath her ridiculous bonnet, catching only the slightest peek at his stubbled jaw, his smooth lips.

Lips she might never know. Never feel them against her own.

Oh, if Arabella knew anything, she knew that would never do.

After handing Birdie up into the carriage, Kingsley turned to his friend. "Augie, a word."

Augie backed up a step or two. "Would love to, but I haven't the time," he declared, turning to flee.

Kingsley caught him by the collar. "A word." "Guiding" him a few steps from the carriage, and out of Birdie's sharp hearing, he asked, nay demanded, "How do you know her?"

"Know who?" Augie glanced this way and that, but most notably not in the lady's direction.

"Demmit, you know very well who I mean. Birdie."

"Ah, Birdie!" Augie's mouth widened into a smile. "Delightful gel. A devil of a handful, but I imagine you have everything in order."

"Who. Is. She?" he bit out.

And to his disbelief, Augie shook his head. "Not mine to tell, my good man." Then he set his mouth in a mulish line.

He'd known Augie since they'd been lads, knew enough of his friend that nothing could induce him to tell what he knew. Augie was nothing if not loyal. So Kingsley let go of him.

Then Augie surprised him again by catching hold of his sleeve and tugging him down so they could see each other eye to eye. "You do anything to ruin her, to break her heart, and I'll put a bullet through your chest."

Kingsley, who had faced the French in a dozen or more engagements, who'd had two horses shot out from beneath him at Quatre Bras, had known fear. But it was nothing like the cold chill that knifed through him now.

The man meant it.

Then Augie released him and in the blink of an eye was back to his usual congenial self. "There now, as I understand it, you owe the lady two more labors." He straightened his jacket and puffed up a bit. "Be about them and then have her home safely." He bowed, then glanced over his shoulder at the carriage. "Mind what I said, Birdie."

She nodded with a regal air. "I promise, Lord Augustus."

With that, Augie waved at Birdie and ambled off, whistling a jaunty tune.

Kingsley turned slowly and gave his full attention to the lady in his carriage. Her smile seemed to tremble a bit, as if she were waiting for some hammer to fall upon her expectations.

Then she sat up straight as if remembering herself, and her chin jutted up just a bit, as if she wasn't about to let anything—or anyone—deter her.

He had no doubt she would be as closemouthed as Augie, so there was no point in wasting his breath and prying as to how some *cit's* daughter knew the youngest son of the Marquess of Prendwick.

"What say you, Birdie? Where are we off to next?" he asked as he climbed up into the driver's seat.

Her eyes widened and then her smile followed suit. "Truly?"

He nodded. "I promised."

"That you did," she said firmly, folding her hands in her lap. "I would like to take tea with someone."

Tea? That wasn't quite what he had expected, but at least it was something that could hardly lead them on the path to ruin.

Augie's warning had rather startled him and he glanced back toward the crowd, half expecting to see his old friend peering after them like a gargoyle of old.

. . . *break her heart, and I'll put a bullet through your chest.*

Never once in all the years he'd known Augie had the man ever left him floored.

But this time, he suspected Augie wasn't joking. Not in the least.

"Tea, is it? That sounds rather tame after a boxing match," Kingsley teased as he gathered up the ribbons and turned the horses toward the city.

"Yes, well, we will need to secure an introduction first."

An introduction? Kingsley paused for a moment. "Who the devil are we taking tea with, the Prince Regent?"

"Oh, no one as boring as all that," she said, as if taking tea with the heir to the throne was a weekly occurrence. "I want to take tea with Mrs. Spenser."

Mrs. Spenser? No, he hadn't heard her correctly.

But when he turned toward her, there it was, her eyes twinkling with mischief.

And worse, a determined sort of challenge.

"Considering the lengths you went to meet her the other night," she said, "you can hardly object to taking tea with her this afternoon, now can you?" She paused and nodded toward the road. A silent nudge to remind him that he'd promised. "Not quite the assignation you planned, I imagine, but I find tea is always a very good beginning to an association, don't you agree?"

They drove for London for some time in silence.

Arabella could tell Kingsley was working on a raft of objections as to why and how they could not just call on London's most infamous courtesan and demand she take tea with them.

And when he did begin listing all the reasons, she was at the ready.

"One doesn't just call on a courtesan," he explained.

"Why not?"

This set his jaw to working back and forth. "Because it isn't done."

"She'll make an exception for us, I am most certain." She smiled brightly. Aunt Josephine always said that confidence in one's opinion, no matter how shaky it might be, would always help buoy a cause.

Yet Kingsley just snorted at her words.

"I thought you wanted to meet her?" she pressed. "I do believe you expressed an interest to get to know her quite intimately."

. . . after I've discovered every delectable, delightful corner of your divine body. . .

Bother the man, but every time Arabella recalled those words, that promise, her body tightened, shivered with a begging need.

No matter how shameless it was, Arabella wondered what it would be like to have Kingsley discover every corner of her body.

Next to her, the major shifted in his seat, as if he was recalling his words as well. "That is neither here nor there," he objected. "Women like Mrs. Spenser don't just let strangers into their homes. There are rules to this sort of thing." He glanced away, while one hand loosened his cravat.

"Rules? What sort of rules?" Arabella shook her head. "And here I thought these ladies had all the freedom in the world."

"They are most particular about who they befriend."

"And how do they choose who they friend?"

"Like anyone else, I suppose," he replied, tugging again at his cravat.

Truly, whatever was wrong with the man? He was making a mess of that linen. "You suppose? Don't you know? Haven't you had a mistress?"

"Good God, Birdie! This is not something one discusses with a lady."

She fluffed her red dress and let her lashes flutter at him. "But I am not a lady. Don't you recall what you told Rollins? A Flemish piece." Now it was her turn to snort. "He isn't very bright, your friend."

At this even Kingsley had to laugh. "No, he is not."

"Flemish, indeed." She turned so he could see her in her entirety. "Do I look Flemish to you?"

"You look like a very expensive handful."

That, for whatever reason delighted her. "Thank you very much." And it wasn't his words that had her feeling grateful, but the wolfish light in his eyes.

And if to confirm his statement, a pair of blades driving out—most likely having learned of the boxing match late—came flying by, but not so fast that one of them hadn't the time to let out a long, appreciative whistle.

"I am acquiring admirers," she crowed. "Is that how it is done?"

"No. The usual method is expensive jewels and a promise of rents paid."

"Jewelry!" Arabella exclaimed. "Why didn't I think of that?"

"What do you mean?" Kingsley asked, a wary wrinkle to his brow.

"Jewelry. We must bring an offering of jewelry. Then Mrs. Spenser will have to invite us to tea. We could bring a basket as well. From Fortnum & Mason, I think, so as not to trouble the lady's staff."

Kingsley made a sort of choking noise. "Just like that, we are adding a trip to Rundell & Bridge and a basket from Fortnum & Mason to ensure our success?"

"Exactly!" she agreed, ignoring the sarcasm in his voice. "And how perfect of you to think of Rundell & Bridge. Are you certain you haven't a mistress?"

"No, I do not have a mistress." He shifted again in his seat and looked away.

Arabella didn't know why, but that bit of information tickled her. So there wasn't a lady somewhere waiting for him—even if there was some unknown lady who was to be his bride.

Might be, she recalled, remembering his denial of any impending nuptials.

Make that *adamant* denial. So, they had that in common.

Further, he'd all but confessed that his heart wasn't engaged elsewhere.

She shouldn't be happy, but she was, for whatever unfathomable reason.

Tipping her bonnet back, she found Major Kingsley studying her, his dark brows furrowed like a freshly turned field.

"What?" she asked, feeling as if she had just grown an extra head.

"If you think I am taking you to Rundell & Bridge, let alone Fortnum & Mason, dressed in that rig, you've gone round the bend."

"But if we are to take tea with Mrs. Spenser—"

"I doubt even Mrs. Spenser would approve of such a gown. Besides, you will outshine the lady—a fact that will not amuse her."

That was rather a mixed compliment, Arabella decided. And however did he know what such ladies preferred?

Worse was the implication that her outing was impossible.

"Pull over," she told him. "Right there." Arabella pointed at the opening in a hedge alongside the road. "That will do perfectly."

"Perfectly for what?" he asked as he guided the horses to a stop.

"To change, of course."

CHAPTER 7

"Change?" Kingsley sputtered. "Right now? Here?"

"Well, I can hardly change my clothes on a London street corner," Birdie shot back. "Besides, you said it was entirely necessary—"

"I don't recall that I ever—" he began, visions of a scantily clad Birdie teasing up in his imagination and leaving him dry-mouthed and speechless.

No. He couldn't think of her thusly. *Naked.*

No, he mustn't.

But it was demmed difficult not to, for here she was reaching under her seat and pulling out the bundled gown—the one she'd been wearing earlier.

"This won't take long," she promised as she hopped down from the curricle and walked—rather swayed—over to the stone fence. That outlandish rig she'd bought couldn't do anything but sway seductively.

He'd held her intimately, closely, that night at the ball. Let his hands roam over her, thinking her experienced and willing. Knew every line that had just sashayed across the road.

Now he regretted such knowledge.

For it made watching her a trial, his hands flexing rest-lessly inside his driving gloves, his body shifting to find a more comfortable position.

She'd made her way to a stile, nearly hidden in the over-grown hedge that grew up around the stones. How'd she'd spotted it he didn't know, but she certainly had an eye for gaining what she needed.

"No peeking," she warned him over her shoulder as she got to the top of the wall. This was followed by a wag of her finger. "Promise?"

"Isn't that adding additional terms to our agreement?"

Her brow wrinkled in consternation. What a funny, mer-curial bit of muslin Birdie was turning out to be. "That term was always implicitly implied," she informed him.

Implicitly implied. Good heavens. He was now firmly con-vinced her father was a barrister. Or a member of Parliament. "If that is your argument—"

"It is," she told him. "Upon your word—"

"As a gentleman," he promised, crossing his finger over his heart.

She nodded in agreement and then turned back to the stile, studying the path of her descent.

At least she hadn't argued the gentleman part. Then again, he wondered what the devil Augie had told her about him.

After a moment of hesitation, weighing the best way down, she gathered up the hem of her outlandish gown, leav-ing her ankles and a good part of her calves in view.

Dear God in heaven! The minx had even gained a pair of red silk stockings out of her bargain with that rag merchant.

Then an even more startling thought struck him—what if those were the stockings she'd been wearing when he'd nearly run her over?

Outlandish chit! He wouldn't put it past her—a demure gown and the most intriguing choices of . . . *unmentionables.*

Kingsley began to cough and sputter.

She paused and glanced back at him. "Whatever is the matter?"

"You," he said, nodding toward her ankles.

Her eyes widened a bit as she glanced down, then she grinned in delight. "Why, thank you." Two steps later, she disappeared over the other side.

Kingsley heaved a sigh and settled back in his seat, taking his hat off and raking a hand through his hair, letting the breeze cool and ruffle his tangled desires.

Truly, there was nothing he could do but wait, and so he let the bucolic scene around him soothe him further. The birds twittering in the hedge. The lowing of cattle off in the distance. He drew in a deep breath of fresh air, filled as it was with the scents of fields and grass, and realized how much he had missed the English countryside.

From over the hedge, a question came fluttering into his thoughts. "Kingsley?"

"Yes, Birdie?"

"Whyever did you agree to my terms?" She hesitated for a second before she continued. "Especially if you are supposed to be elsewhere?"

He searched for an answer and replied the only away he could. Honestly. "I don't know. And yes."

For a time the only reply was the chirping of sparrows in the hedge.

"Will you still have to go? Elsewhere, that is?"

The wistful note to her words tugged at him. "Yes. Just as I suppose you must as well."

Another pause and then there was a rustle in the hedge. Over the top of the brambles came her red gown.

Kingsley stilled. There it was fluttering in the breeze like a regiment's standard, that red color calling for one and all to muster.

He certainly was. Mustering, that is. His chest contracted, damned well tightened to the point where he could barely breathe. Hell, all of him tightened.

I am a gentleman, he reminded himself. And while she'd made him promise not to look, that didn't mean his imagination couldn't run wild.

Visions of that gown tossed on the floor of his bedchamber . . . Birdie naked in his bed . . .

And when one of the red stockings came floating atop the gown, Kingsley's heart galloped as if called to action.

The other stocking followed the first. "I hardly want our day to end."

And neither did he, Kingsley realized, much to his own shock. His gaze strayed back to the stile. The path that led to her. To hell. To redemption.

To a bullet in his chest, if he believed Augie.

After a few more minutes of rustling and muttering, she spoke again. "Oh, bother!"

"What is it?"

"I can't manage the hooks. They are all in the back."

"That is a dilemma," Kingsley replied, trying not to laugh. Nor conjure up an image of a half-clad Birdie.

But despite his best efforts—well, perhaps not his *best*—visions of her discarded gown teased him. Called to him to come closer.

He did his best to end his imaginings there.

A deep and resolute sigh rose up from her hiding spot. "You'll need to help me."

"Help?" he managed, the word nearly strangling him. It stuck like Augie's threat, lodging coldly in his chest.

Ruin her and I'll put a bullet through your chest.

"Yes, help," she continued. "How else am I to get dressed? Not unless you have a lady's maid tucked into your traveling trunk."

"But—"

"Oh, bother, Kingsley. You'll just have to come over to the hedge." It wasn't a request, but an order.

Taking a deep breath, Kingsley straightened his shoulders. Girded himself, in a sense. He could do this. Why, it was nothing, what she was asking. Do up a few buttons and hooks.

Yes, nothing at all.

Tying off the reins, he climbed down. Then yanking off his gloves, Kingsley tossed them up on the seat. Bare-handed like one of the pugilists they'd left behind, he stalked across the road toward the stile.

Instead of having the sense of going to battle, he rather felt like he was wading into a storm-swollen river.

One of unknown depths. Capable of drowning a man in an instant.

Rather like a come-hither glance from her blue eyes.

Oh, he was going to regret this.

"No peeking," she admonished from somewhere on the other side.

His boot froze over the first step. "How am I supposed to get over to the other side without looking?" After a moment or two, he added, "Or without breaking my neck?"

"Close your eyes," she instructed.

"Close my—"

"Just close them," she told him. There was a snap to her words that held an aristocratic air he well recognized. Why, his own father could bite out a single command that instantly had half the county jumping to do his bidding.

"Are your eyes closed?"

Kingsley shuttered them. For if he died here on the side of the road, there was some consolation that his untimely and utterly scandalous demise would completely thwart his autocratic father's designs. "Now what?"

"Hold out your hand."

He did, and almost immediately her much smaller paw caught hold of him. Her fingers were soft and silky as they twined with his, but when they closed around him he felt her strength, her will, holding him steady.

"Now, take another step up."

He did as he was bid, but his boot hit the step and he nearly pitched forward. But there was Birdie, anchoring him in place.

"Higher," she told him. "Lift your foot higher."

He did, and soon she had him up and over the other side, his feet landing in the soft earth with a heavy thud.

With his eyes closed, his other senses filled in the gaps. The soft breeze rustling across his face, the trilling chatter of the birds in the hedges, while leaves whispered to one another as they danced and swayed overhead.

And a whiff of something tempting. A bit of roses and a bit exotic and utterly female.

Birdie.

"Now," she began, "the hooks are up the back—I can't get them around the buttons."

"You expect me to do this with my eyes closed?" He laughed at the utter irony of it, for he was more of an expert in undoing such hindrances, not the other way around.

"It can't be that difficult," she told him. "Just reach out a bit. I am right in front of you."

And tentatively his hand came up and reached out until his fingers brushed into the bare skin of her back. The moment he touched her, she jumped.

"Sorry—" he began.

"No, no. It's just your hand is—" She stopped there. And then, as if remembering that this was her idea, she eased back into his hand, his fingers splaying out over her soft, warm skin.

When she shivered, trembled beneath him, he was nearly undone. That, and he swore she'd just moved closer. Inviting him to . . .

Oh, good God! He couldn't think such things. Give in to such temptation.

All he needed was Augie to happen along on this scene. And then his friend could make good his vow before Kingsley had a chance to even offer an explanation.

Not that he thought for a second that Augie would listen to anything he could manage to sputter out in his own defense.

"Perhaps," the little temptress in front of him began, speaking tentatively, as if struggling to find the words. "If you opened your eyes—"

Open them? Oh, now there was the devil's own tangle.

Yet it wasn't like his better senses were holding sway. His eyes opened before he could find a good argument against such a course.

But truly, if he could see what he was doing, this task would be over in a snap and they could be back in the relative safety of an open carriage on a public thoroughfare.

Then he looked at the sight before him. Even in the shadowy enclosure of the hedges, he could see the rosy flush of her fair skin, the faint fluttering of her pulse in her neck. She'd removed her hat, so for the first time he could truly see her hair, chestnut and rich, with hints of fire, like the lady herself.

She was holding her hair up so it was out of his way, like some Titian beauty in repose, half waiting, and entirely tempting.

Yes, there it was. Having his eyes open wasn't going to make any part of this easier.

"The buttons?" she whispered. No, more like nudged.

"Oh, yes," he replied, pulling his hand back and remembering himself. His promise.

More to the point, Augie's vow.

His fingers had never felt as clumsy as they were trying to catch the tiny pearl buttons and slip them into the loops where they belonged. In his estimation, lady's maids were certainly underpaid, for this was no easy task.

Especially with the added distraction of the lady herself.

It struck him that this was something no man had ever seen before—the curve of her shoulder blades as they made a valley down her back. One that begged to be traced with his fingers, his lips . . .

He reached for the last button and paused, and as he hesitated, she turned slightly, having mistaken his distraction as a sign that the task was completed.

But it was too much, for she was so close, his senses filled with her scent, the silk of her skin, the brush of her skirt against his legs each time she swayed.

And it wasn't just him, but her as well. For Birdie had that rare light in her eyes that no man ever mistakes. One filled with desire, with fire, with need.

She tipped her chin up toward him, almost defiantly. Her lips parted, slowly, ever so slightly. As if daring him to give in to his desires.

"Kingsley?"

"Yes, Birdie?"

"Will you teach me . . . ?"

"Teach you?"

She hesitated as she glanced at his lips. "To whistle, that is."

"Oh, aye, yes," he said, letting out a breath that for whatever reason he'd been holding.

He didn't even have to reach for her, she was there, right in his arms even as his hand rose to cradle her chin. He reached with his other to pluck at something—a bit of a twig from the hedge—that was stuck in her hair, tossing it aside and then casting with it his last remaining bit of restraint.

Whistling, indeed.

He bent his head and brushed her lips with his. It was slight and brief, yet that moment of contact, of touch, of tentative exploration, shifted his world. He was in that swollen river, the one he'd meant to avoid. Yet here he was, drowning, and her lips were the very oxygen his lungs begged for, needed, desired over anything else.

There was nothing he could do but kiss her yet again.

Arabella hadn't thought he would.

Kiss her, that is.

For all his protestations of being a gentleman, she was ever so delighted to discover that he wasn't *that* much of one.

No, he was a rake and a scoundrel. At least she had to assume so, given the way just the merest brush of his lips against her sent her senses a-tumble.

Oh, dear heavens, she was lost. That faint tolling, that whisper of desire, that had echoed through her since the night of the ball—the one this devil had awakened—now clamored to life.

His lips, hard and sure, covered hers, surrounded her, demanding surrender.

She was a Tremont, through and through, so surrender wasn't part of her vocabulary, but passion was . . .

And right now, this rogue was coaxing and teasing that very Tremont part of her, blowing on that dangerous ember that got her notorious family into so much trouble when it blazed to life.

Kingsley continued to kiss her, surely and deeply, his tongue swiping at her lips, opening her.

Her fingers twined in the lapels of his coat, and she pulled him closer. For suddenly she couldn't be close enough to him, even with her body rocking against his, curving into him like a cat.

And what she discovered, what she found herself up against, did not disappoint.

The major was hard, and long, and muscled. For a fleeting moment she wondered what he had looked like in his regimentals.

Then she wondered what he'd look like out of them . . .

That came to her, even as her hands moved over his chest. She wanted to see those smooth, solid planes bared. So she could put her hand over his heart and let it hammer steadily beneath her palm.

That sense of throbbing, the desires his kiss was pulling from her left her dizzy, breathless.

His kiss, hungry and hurried, suddenly slowed, as if he were savoring something he'd never known, had just discovered.

And for her as well. Instead of her world spinning so out of control, everything slowed to a single moment.

Arabella, inexperienced as she was, knew something so very fundamental had changed in the blink of an eye.

Like the beat of Kingsley's heart beneath her fingers.

His kiss turned almost reverent, his touch gentle and filled with a startling intimacy.

Arabella moved closer, her fingers grasping at him, trying to stop time.

So it is, so it is time. The words came out of nowhere. Warned her.

That thread, the one she knew could be so easily broken, now tightened around them, winding its way around her heart, whispering as it coiled and teased its way deeper and deeper.

It will never be like this with anyone else.

This kiss. His touch.

This very passion.

The heated, tempestuous one racing through her as he cupped her, drew her closer, had her standing on her tiptoes so she could rise higher, catch hold of this delicious passion, all before it returned to the heavens.

And yet, the more he touched her, the more she knew he would only mark her deeper, leave her with memories of a passion that would never be fulfilled.

Now that passion turned to terror, as suddenly all Arabella could feel, all she could see was the emptiness of the future.

Days and months and years with only the memory of Kingsley's kiss.

And of a promise that would never be kept. Never found.

With a will she'd never had to summon, she broke free of his kiss, his grasp.

But she doubted she would ever be able to break the hold on her heart he'd managed to gain in those few, heavenly moments.

Kingsley pulled in a deep breath and tried to clear his thoughts, as Birdie broke away from him, her eyes wide with shock and the rest of her . . .

Well, the rest of her was a sensuous feast to behold. Her lips half open, her tousled hair, her gown still just a bit askew.

But there was no invitation in her glance, and he suspected he knew why.

Something had changed between them.

And thankfully Birdie had been smart enough to break the spell.

Kingsley wasn't sure he'd have had the wherewithal.

For just that reason—something *had* changed.

No wonder Augie had warned him off.

The girl was fire and magic and temptation, all at once.

"We should be going back to London," Birdie was saying, having shaken out her skirt and twisted her hair back under her bonnet. She'd found her way to the stile and had one foot resting on the step.

When he nodded in agreement—for he didn't trust himself to speak—she went up and over, like a sparrow taking flight.

It wasn't until they had gotten nearly to the carriage that Kingsley finally found something to say, yet even as the question came tumbling out, it shocked even him.

"This man, the one your father is insisting you marry, what do you know of him?"

Is he good enough for you? was what he was really asking.

She stilled, standing at the side of the carriage, and she spoke without looking at him. "He was in the military—like you."

He untied the horses and made his way to his side—for Birdie had already scrambled up to her seat.

"Perhaps he was a hero—" Kingsley suggested, even as he tried to consider who this unknown swain might be.

At this she barked a bit of a laugh. "Hardly," she said. "He most likely manned a very comfortable desk somewhere far from the lines. Certainly not like you. You were at Waterloo. I imagine you're the hero."

"Me?" This took Kingsley back a bit. "I was no hero. I merely managed to stay alive."

Finally she turned toward him. "You were wounded."

The admiration in her eyes took him aback. "That doesn't make me a hero," he demurred, "simply because I got in the way of an errant French bullet."

"You weren't shot . . ." She glanced downward, her head tipping, and immediately he understood her implication.

"Birdie! You aren't suggesting that I was shot in the—"

She blushed, but still her gaze stayed firmly planted on his backside.

"No," he said, shifting around so she couldn't look at him like that. "I wasn't shot *there*."

"Then where were you shot?"

"That is hardly a question one asks."

"Then I will just continue with my original theory," she told him, a mischievous light in her eyes, and her head tilted again as her gaze drifted downward.

"Enough," he told her. "Oh, good God! If you must know, I was shot in the shoulder. It wasn't much. Not compared to what others suffered, endured." He climbed into his seat and took up the reins even as he thought of his friend Christopher, an aide to Wellington, and how his arm had been lost— blown away by the shards from a cannonball.

"Does it pain you much?" she asked.

"Not as much as your incessant questions."

And if he had thought that would stem her boundless curiosity, he was very wrong.

Birdie laughed and settled back in her seat, her face turned toward the road ahead. "Then if your injuries are beyond what is proper to discuss, do tell me about the Continent. I am ever so jealous of your travels."

"You wouldn't be if you had seen the conditions of some of the Italian inns I stayed in."

"Perhaps," she conceded. "But they are in *Italy*."

And with that, he couldn't argue.

Kingsley entertained her with tales of his travels the rest of the way into London. Better to chatter on about Italian architecture, traveling woes, and the odd haunts he'd found along the way than discuss what had happened back in that bower.

What shouldn't have happened, he reminded himself.

And yet . . . what the devil had happened?

One moment he'd been kissing her, holding her, touching her, and then suddenly everything had shifted, his passion had moved from mere heat and desire, to a need that strangled his heart. He hadn't wanted to just kiss her, he'd wanted to cherish every moment.

He'd wanted that kiss never to end.

And that terrified him more than standing in the middle of a battlefield, unhorsed and with cannonballs exploding all around him. Death had a finality about it, but what he'd felt kissing this minx had a different sort of finality about it.

As if he'd just discovered the only woman he was meant to love.

Birdie? No! It was impossible, for so many reasons. Starting with the very fact that he had no idea who she was.

He knew now she was educated, passionate, and quick-witted, for she wasn't averse to arguing history and art, and when he described the sights of Venice, she'd stilled, her eyes wide with a mixture of awe and joy.

The question she'd asked him earlier, *Would you go back?* began nudging at him.

And now it had a different sort of undertone. Would he want to retrace his steps across the Continent with her at his side?

For a moment he considered doing just that—turning the carriage toward the Dover road and taking the first packet across the Channel.

And then what? he asked himself.

Spend a few delightful months exploring Paris and the Alps and Rome and Vesuvius, and, of course, Birdie?

Save for one simple fact: he hadn't the blunt. With every farthing of the inheritance from his grandfather gone, he could no longer do as his heart desired.

Desire.

Beside him, Birdie stirred in her seat, adjusting her bonnet, and a hint of her perfume wafted past his nose.

Tempting. Passionate. Teasing. All at once.

Still, he couldn't help wondering what would it be like to take her by the hand and show her Venice. Let her breathe in the mingling of history, and faraway seas, and languages filled with life . . .

A vision of a small, comfortable suite of rooms on the *Rio de la Madoneta* teased into his thoughts. Of the large bed in the upper room, the one that afforded views of the Grand Canal.

Of time. Of all the time and solitude two people could ever desire. Need. Want.

"Whatever are you considering?" she asked, barging into his woolgathering.

"Something wicked," he confessed.

"No doubt," she shot back, arms crossing over her chest. "You have the most faraway expression on your face . . ."

"I was far away."

"Where were you?"

"Venice." After a moment, he added, "If I could take you—"

Her eyes narrowed. "That would be madness."

Her remark might have been intended to be a scold, but he wondered if perhaps she was saying it more for her own benefit than his.

"Yes, I suppose it would be."

"And impossible," she pointed out as they crossed New Bridge Street, and Fleet Street became Ludgate Hill. The staid and elegant shop of Rundell & Bridge came into view.

"As impossible as knocking on Mrs. Spenser's door and inviting ourselves to tea?" he teased.

"With the right gift, she will hardly refuse us," she told him with every confidence.

As the carriage came to a stop outside the shop, Kingsley had to wonder at the wisdom of this—going into one of the *ton*'s most respected and exclusive jewelers.

Someone was going to recognize him.

And when they did, the afternoon mail would have more than its fair share of notes traveling off to the Abbey, each filled with an *on dit* that would age his mother and put his father into apoplexy.

Your son was seen outside Rundell & Bridge with a young lady. . .

He glanced over at Birdie and wondered what his parents would make of her—with her outspoken ways, outlandish desires, and lofty sense of self-worth.

Kingsley nearly grinned. Ah, the very solid and ancient stones of the Abbey would tumble down around them in outrage.

"Are you going in, milord?" the boy at the curb called out. He wasn't one of the usual ragtag lads who held horses for gentleman, but one of Rundell's own lads, smartly suited and tidy as the shop window itself.

"Yes, I believe we are," Kingsley told him. Better to get inside than continue to sit out here in the street on public display. Already they were garnering curious glances from passersby. He turned to Birdie, awaiting her confirmation, only to discover that he wasn't the only one worried about being recognized.

The chit who had worn that outrageous red gown like a banner now had her bonnet pulled low so that it nearly covered her face.

Good God, she didn't want to be seen any more than he did.

Perhaps more so . . .

Then again, hadn't her father proven how far he would go to keep his daughter's reputation pure?

Kingsley gingerly rubbed his still tender eye, as a reminder and a talisman.

He'd been convinced that night, after realizing she wasn't

some infamous courtesan, that she was most likely the daughter of some enterprising and social-climbing mushroom. For her beauty and virtue (and what was probably a very large dowry) would make up for her lack of noble connections.

After all, the Setchfield ball was known for being far more democratic than exclusive.

But suddenly this assumption took a turn.

If she didn't want anyone recognizing her, who was she?

"Birdie?" Kingsley prompted, trying a different tack. "Have you changed your mind? There is no reason why we can't just go to Gunter's for ices."

That did the trick.

"Gunter's?" She shook her head vehemently. "Oh, dear, no." She turned toward the jewelry shop, her brow furrowing for a moment. "Is it the expense? While I haven't the money on me, I will be more than happy to see your costs for today reimbursed."

He laughed. "No, it isn't the expense."

"That's good because I wasn't sure how I was going to manage that," she confessed. "I suspect Mrs. Spenser is most familiar with a box tied in their red ribbon—so she will know immediately we are not gaping paupers. That, and any other shop would just seem inferior."

"Inferior?" He laughed a bit. His Birdie was quite the connoisseur. "We could hardly offer our conquest an 'inferior' gift."

"Exactly," she agreed, once again missing the teasing note to his words. "Though I have no desire to put you into a debt."

"I thought I already was . . . in your debt, that is." If he was ever going to discover who this little siren might be, the only thing to do was to keep playing along with her outlandish requests.

Besides, there was a wry part of him that rather liked putting some bauble on his father's account.

One last defiant act, he decided.

He tossed the reins to the boy, who caught them smartly, and then got down and ambled around the carriage. "Come along, Birdie, my girl. Let us buy an offering for this goddess you so dearly want to meet."

CHAPTER 8

"Who is at the door, Peg?"

"A Major Kingsley."

"Kingsley, Kingsley . . ." Justina Spenser bit her lip and went through the lists of names she'd memorized through necessity from *Debrett's*. When that failed to offer any clue, she did a running recount of the latest gossip columns, and then it came to her.

Kingsley. Good heavens . . .

"Why, he's the heir of—" Her fleet mind began to calculate at having such a young and rich admirer.

New curtains. Carpets.

Peg knew exactly what she was doing and only added to the temptation by holding out a package. "Whoever he is, he sent this."

The familiar box and ribbon told all too clearly where the tempting offering inside had come from.

Rundell & Bridge.

Tasteful *and* expensive.

With quick fingers—for this wasn't the first time she'd

opened such a gift—Justina unwrapped the offering and was delighted to find an exquisite silver bracelet, worked to look like oak leaves twining around the wearer's wrist. Dangling from it were small acorns decorated with tiny gems.

"Oh, my," Peg wheezed. "I didn't expect that."

Mrs. Spenser looked up from the bracelet. "Why not?"

"This Kingsley brought a young lady with him."

"A wha-a-a-t?"

"A young lady," Peg repeated. "A right proper one, if my eyes don't deceive me."

Mrs. Spenser saw no reason to argue the matter. If Peg said the girl was quality, she most likely was. "What do they want?"

Peg snorted. "Some prattle about taking tea with you, if it isn't too much bother."

"Take tea?" This time Mrs. Spenser was the parrot, for she couldn't quite believe what she was hearing.

"Oh, aye, take tea. Brought a basket with them as well, so it wouldn't be a bother." Peg shook her head as if she'd never seen such foolishness, but just as quickly her eyes narrowed. "That basket will feed us for a week, it will. Keep the green-grocer off our back step."

Practical to a fault was Peg.

"Send them up," Mrs. Spenser ordered, taking one more covetous glance inside the box before she snapped the lid closed.

"Both of them?" Peg made a disapproving *tsk, tsk*.

"Whatever is the matter?"

"I didn't think you were inclined that way."

She wasn't, but her gaze flitted again toward the box.

"Oh, who am I chiding." Peg laughed with a wheeze. "You'd sleep with Wellington's horse for that bauble."

She might, but that was neither here nor there. "You said they just want to have tea?"

"Yes, an introduction and tea."

"And you say she's quality?" Mrs. Spenser shook her head at the suggestion. "You must be mistaken. He wouldn't dare bring a girl of noble birth to see me."

Peg got that calculating look in her eye. One old courtesan past her prime to a lady who was in the midst of her best years. "Care to wager?"

"Yes."

"My pearl ear bobs," Peg offered. They were the last of her retirement jewels, and she had held on to the fat, glossy jewels with the greed of Midas.

"Done! Against your wages for the next month—"

"Two," Peg said, raising the stakes.

"Yes, if you insist, two months," Justina said, waving her hand at the entire suggestion as if it were she who was granting some grand favor. Hardly, when they both knew those ear bobs would easily bring a year's worth of wages.

"And *all* my wages, Justina," Peg told her, one graying brow cocked up in indignation. "Including the portion you skim off when Lord Trumble gives them to you."

"Welcome, welcome," Mrs. Spenser said in an elegantly accented voice.

If Kingsley had to guess, he'd say she exhibited hints of an upper-crust education and a dash of French nobility. Or that was at least the impression the lady wanted to convey.

And the same with her legendary beauty—she was a decidedly handsome woman, with dark auburn hair, a fair complexion, and a tall, willowy figure that curved precisely as it ought. But what made the infamous Incognita stand out was her eyes—quick and sharp, giving no doubt to anyone of the intelligence behind them and a defiant independence that would not be easily dominated.

No wonder her admirers were politicians and artists and the very upper reaches of Society.

"How kind of you to come and call on me." She said this with a grand smile, as if their visit was just the pleasant surprise of old friends arriving unexpectedly. "Peg, dear, do fetch a pot of tea," she asked of the crone who had answered the door.

"Oh, aye, ma'am," Peg replied with a bit of a snort to her words and her eyes alight with a curious sparkle.

"Mrs. Spenser, I must apologize for our thoughtless intrusion upon your hospitality," Birdie rushed to say as Mrs. Spenser led them into her parlor, a room that looked out not on the garden like most London homes, but on the fashionable promenade below. "I rather insisted to poor Major Kingsley to bring me here."

"Poor Major Kingsley, indeed!" Mrs. Spenser laughed. "It is Major Kingsley, isn't it?" The woman eyed him as one might a questionable stone in a necklace.

"Yes, Major Kingsley, madam," he replied, making an elegant bow.

"Yes, I can see that now," Mrs. Spenser said, slanting a bemused glance at him that suggested she was willing to play along—for now. Then she turned to his companion. "And you, my dear girl, who might you be?"

"Birdie, ma'am."

Mrs. Spenser tipped her head and studied her like a curiosity. "Birdie, eh? Taken flight, have we?"

"In a sense," Birdie replied, holding her own.

Mrs. Spenser sat down on a settee, and patted the seat next to her for Birdie to share. Once the ladies were seated, Kingsley took the grand chair across from them, the only chair in the room that seemed designed for a man.

A regal, comfortable throne for her chosen patron. Oh, yes, there was no doubt in his mind that Mrs. Spenser was a sharp and intelligent woman.

And with the two of them seated side by side, Kingsley was struck by how similar they were in manners—hands poised in their laps, shoulders straight, and smiles at the ready.

Though he did catch Birdie slanting curious glances around the salon as if looking for some sign of iniquity in this tastefully appointed room. He nearly laughed when a flicker of disappointment flashed across her brow.

Meanwhile, Mrs. Spenser smiled warmly at both of them. "However did the two of you fall into company? And whatever has brought you to my doorstep?" She looked from Kingsley to Birdie and then back to the major. For this last glance, her brow rose ever so slightly with disapproval.

But her true question—the one behind her words—hadn't escaped him. What the lady really wanted to know was: *What the devil are you doing bringing a respectable young lady to my house?*

"We met at the Setchfield ball," Birdie told her, blithely unaware of the undercurrents.

Or, being Birdie, ignoring them completely.

The lady threw back her head and laughed. "Ah, of course. Such folly and fun to be found there. Every year a new scandal. I take it you two are this year's *on dit?*" The lady's hand rose slightly to brush at her eye, indicating she'd noticed his fading bruise. "Unfortunately, I couldn't attend this year," she told them, "but obviously I missed a grand evening."

"Not in the least," Birdie rushed to tell her.

"No, no," Mrs. Spenser said, waving aside her consolations. "I'm most certain there is quite the scandalous story behind how you two met."

"By chance," Kingsley told her.

"Chance!" the lady scoffed. "No such thing." Mrs. Spenser paused and looked over at Birdie. "Fate guided the two of you together. I am certain."

"I hardly think—" he began, shifting uncomfortably.

Mrs. Spenser ignored him completely. "I would guess you two fell in love. Love at first sight, I imagine. And now your parents disapprove of the match and you've run away. Is that it?"

"No!"

"Most decidedly not!"

These two declarations came out simultaneously, as did the acrimonious glares that followed.

Mrs. Spenser clapped her hands together, grinning over her hands, which where folded as if in prayer at her chin. "To which part?"

"Whatever do you mean?" Birdie asked her.

"Which part of my theory is wrong? Certainly you found Major Kingsley excessively handsome when you met him. Did you not?"

"He's not unimpressive," Birdie said, glancing yet again around the room.

And not at him.

Mrs. Spenser's eyes twinkled. "And you, Major Kingsley? Did you find Birdie enchanting when you first spied her?"

His jaw worked back and forth. "I was under the impression she was someone else."

Mrs. Spenser snorted. "That did not answer my question, but from your tone, I will surmise you found her lovely to behold." The lady looked up. "Ah, Peg! The pot of tea. Such perfect timing."

Her maid came in with the tray, and settled it down on the table before them, the cups rattling as she deposited it. "Now for some refreshments. Birdie, will you please pour, while Major Kingsley regales me with the rest of what I am certain is a love story in the making."

Birdie slanted a warning glance at him as she reached for the teapot. She began to pour as any highborn lady would— perfectly seated, careful not to spill, and holding the pot just so. She did it as if she were a duchess entertaining the queen.

This was no *cit*'s daughter. No solicitor's child. No mushroom's precious hope to rise in Society.

And when he looked up, he found Mrs. Spenser studying not Birdie, but him.

So you noticed as well, her glance seemed to say.

Meanwhile, Birdie had filled in the silence with her own

version of the events. "Our association is nothing more than Major Kingsley kindly offering to escort me through a day's worth of sightseeing."

Kingsley let out a derisive snort. *Kindly offering.*

That was akin to saying the French "kindly" yielded the field at Waterloo.

Birdie's lips pursed together. "I might have implied that he owed me a favor."

"A favor?" Kingsley sputtered.

"Three," Birdie quickly amended.

"Three boons! How utterly delightful," Mrs. Spenser enthused as if there wasn't a hint of tension in the room. "So very Herculean." She took a cup of tea from Birdie, smiling graciously. "What have you asked of poor Major Kingsley? He hasn't had to slay anything or anyone, has he?"

"Not yet," he muttered as he accepted a cup from Birdie. For a second their fingers brushed against each other, and in that brief contact, it happened again.

As it had in the bower. As it had when he'd kissed her. The world seemed to still as if waiting for him to realize that this, this magic, was his for the taking.

If he was willing . . .

Suddenly he was back in that secluded spot by the side of the road and she was once again in his arms, her lips on his, her lithesome body up against him, and all he'd wanted was to . . .

He nearly dropped his teacup when he looked up and found both ladies studying him. Birdie looking murderous and Mrs. Spenser with a knowing smile turning her lips.

"Yes, well, you were about to tell our hostess about your

day—" He blew on his tea and then made a show of stirring the two lumps of the sugar she'd added.

He hadn't asked for any, but Birdie had put them in anyway.

How she'd known, he didn't want to hazard a guess. But one word did prod at his chest.

Fate.

"Major Kingsley took me to the boxing match," Birdie announced.

"The boxing match?" Mrs. Spenser asked, sounding a bit shocked. Considering this was London's most notorious courtesan, Kingsley was surprised anything took the woman aback. "Not the bout with Wilson and Cormack?"

Oh, how wrong he was. The lady was hardly shocked, more like jealous.

"I adore boxing," Mrs. Spenser added on her next breath.

"You do?" Birdie leaned forward.

"Decidedly," the woman declared, leaning forward as well. "How did Wilson appear?"

"In good form," Birdie told her, and in an instant the pair of them had their heads together, discussing the sport with unrivaled enthusiasm.

"What did you think, Major Kingsley?" Mrs. Spenser asked. "Was Wilson in as rare a form as Birdie opines?"

"I wouldn't really know. I've been away so long—"

Mrs. Spenser turned to Birdie. "He was far too distracted by your beauty to notice the fight."

"I was—" he began, only to have Birdie pick up the story and carry it forward, much to Mrs. Spenser's delight.

"He actually told his friend I was Flemish and that I spoke not a word of English."

Mrs. Spenser began to laugh, so much so, she had to put her cup and saucer down. "I'm certain Lord Kingsley only meant—"

"Major Kingsley," he corrected.

Mrs. Spenser sat back. "If you say so—"

"I do," he told her.

The lady nodded slightly, conceding the point.

For now.

Then it struck him. The wily courtesan knew exactly who he was.

Instead of giving him pause—that sent his thoughts moving in another direction. Birdie's. If Mrs. Spenser knew who he was, she must have an excellent notion as to who the lady seated next to her might be.

Kingsley sat up, feeling the tide shift slightly in his favor. Birdie had more to lose in this game than he did—and right now she sat like a robin out on a fence post—cocky and cheeky—but more to the point, unwitting game for the hawk.

Oh, Birdie wouldn't be sitting there, all smug and superior, when this all-too-shrewd woman turned her velvet-clad talons in her direction.

"Now, Birdie, what was your second task for our reluctant hero?" Mrs. Spenser was asking.

"Why, to meet you, of course."

"Me?" Mrs. Spenser's hand went to her heart. "Oh, I am honored."

"I hope we haven't been too presumptuous—" Birdie continued. "Some people were of the opinion that such a request just isn't done."

"It was entirely too presumptuous," the lady told her, but it was hardly a scold. "However, your company is most diverting."

"Thank you, Mrs. Spenser." The minx slanted a glance at him that rang triumphant.

But not for long.

"You are most welcome, Lady—" Mrs. Spenser paused as one might if searching to recall a name.

Birdie's mouth opened almost instantly, as if lulled into doing so by their hostess's purring tones, but she caught herself just as her lips were about to form the name that would be her undoing.

After taking a slow breath, she replied, "Just Birdie, ma'am."

"If you say so," Mrs. Spenser replied, nibbling on a cake.

"I do," Birdie insisted, and when she finally slanted her glance in his direction, he hoped she knew exactly what he was thinking.

Ha, you slippery little minx. She nearly caught you out.

Oh, she did, for she went back to pouring tea with all the attention of a girl just out of the schoolroom.

"Where did you learn to pour, Birdie?" Mrs. Spenser asked. Her voice was again all soothing honey. "At a school, I imagine, and if I were to guess, at Miss Emery's in Bath."

Birdie's lashes sprang open at the very suggestion.

Miss Emery's? Even Kingsley knew that was one of England's most exclusive finishing schools, and only the best of the *ton* attended.

Hell, even his own mother had gone to Miss Emery's in

her long-ago girlhood—something she never failed to mention when she was in company she considered beneath her.

But Birdie? At Miss Emery's? Certainly Mrs. Spenser was wrong. She must be. Birdie might—heavy emphasis on *might*—be well-connected, but lofty enough for Miss Emery's? Hardly.

Yet here was Birdie stumbling along and asking, "How did you know?"

Now it was his turn to gape, not that he did for long, for there was Mrs. Spenser smiling like a cat in the cream.

For he'd been all too correct, she knew exactly who Birdie was—oh, the devil take the woman—for he suspected she'd never tell.

Mrs. Spenser leaned back. "Because I went there as well." And then she waited for the response.

"You did?" Birdie's eyes widened.

Kingsley had managed to stop himself before asking the same incredulous question.

Mrs. Spenser nodded—for both their benefit. "I did. I fear I was sent home my second year."

Now it was Birdie's turn to grin. "I only lasted a year. Barely that, I must admit."

"You never said it was *Miss Emery's* School—" Kingsley pointed out, and then snapped his mouth shut, already regretting the hasty response that had sprung from his lips.

Mrs. Spenser reached for another cake. "I do believe you've shocked poor Major Kingsley."

With both ladies looking at him, mirrored images of mischief and delight in their eyes, Kingsley hadn't felt so outnumbered since Spain.

"Hardly," he remarked, doing his best to appear worldly and unaffected, but inside his thoughts were awhirl.

Who the devil was Birdie?

"Oh, I don't think he's shocked—I fear my exploits are quite tame beside his," Birdie told her new bosom-bow. "Besides, I can't have him discovering all my secrets—not until we've finished one more task . . . Oh, and he's teaching me to whistle."

"To whistle?" Mrs. Spenser pursed her lips and blew a jaunty tune, all merry and full of fun.

Birdie sighed with envy. "Oh! That is ever so delightful. Who taught you?"

At this, Mrs. Spenser's expression changed. "My brother. When we were children."

"I never had a brother or a sister. Well, I haven't had, not until lately."

Mrs. Spenser glanced over at Kingsley as if to nudge him. *Did you gather that bit?*

But all Kingsley could see was Birdie, caged in a high citadel, her overprotective father like a dragon at the base, blowing smoke and fire at all who dared draw near, while the lovely maiden above, lively and passionate, could only gaze out at the world beyond.

His mysterious little miss picked up the teapot and poured a measure more for their hostess and then more for him. "The next time you see your brother, Mrs. Spenser, you must thank him. He did you a grand turn by teaching you so well."

The lady looked away, and there was, for a moment, a dark light in her eyes, a shade drawn.

"I'm so sorry," Birdie rushed to say. "You do see him, don't you? He hasn't . . . He isn't gone?"

She shook her head. "Nothing like, my dear girl. It is just I haven't seen my family in a very long time."

"Oh," Birdie managed, glancing over at Kingsley for a bit of help. "I'm ever so sorry."

"There are times when I am as well," Mrs. Spenser told her, adding a bit of cream to her tea. "But not today. Not when I have such lively and diverting company." The lady's smile returned, and any trace of regret was set aside.

Kingsley guessed it was a skill she'd been forced to learn.

"Now, you were saying you had three tasks for our dear Major Kingsley and this day is drawing to a close," she offered, sending a glance toward the window, where the light was beginning to withdraw. Wrapping her shawl around her shoulders, she glanced at both of them. "So you must indulge me. Whatever is your third task for Major Kingsley?"

"I'd prefer not to say," Birdie told her.

Something about the way she chose her words so carefully said all too clearly he wasn't going to like it. Kingsley had no doubt she didn't want to give him any time to come up with a perfectly argued protest as to why whatever harebrained notion she'd come up with was utterly impossible.

Such as taking tea with a courtesan.

Nor was Mrs. Spenser inclined to pry. For she rose from her seat. "Now, my dear Birdie, since we will not meet again—"

"But of course we—"

"No," Mrs. Spenser told her in all certainty, "you mustn't return. It wouldn't be proper, would it, Major Kingsley?" The lady shot him a censorious glance that said all too clearly he should have known as much to begin with.

"No, Birdie. It wouldn't be prudent."

"There," Mrs. Spenser declared, sweeping away at her skirts. "We are all in agreement. This afternoon is our secret." She turned toward the door. "That includes you, Peg."

There was a muttered acknowledgement from just beyond the door.

"I love her dearly, my Peg," Mrs. Spenser said with a sigh of resignation, "but she is as mad as they come. Why, she told me you were a nobleman, Major Kingsley, and that you, my dear Birdie, were a highborn lady." Her eyes alight with mischief, she smiled at both of them. "A truly ridiculous notion, wouldn't you both agree?"

Arabella tried to breathe. *A highborn lady?* She didn't dare look at Kingsley for fear he'd see the truth in her eyes.

Then again, what had Mrs. Spenser said about him? *A nobleman.* Now she couldn't resist a peek at the man.

This time when she looked at Kingsley, she set aside everything she'd merely decided about him and tried to see him as she might have had they met at a soiree or in the park.

The strong Roman features, the set of his shoulders, his hawklike expression. Yes, he had a military stamp to him, but he also carried himself with an unmistakable air of nobility.

Oh, had she not seen it? But then again, she realized she had known—at some level—all along that Kingsley was a gentleman.

Despite that he kissed like a rake . . .

"Come along, Birdie. It is time we ladies had a moment alone. Besides, Major Kingsley has been eyeing those last three cakes and he's too polite simply to take them."

Birdie glanced over at Kingsley—and found him wearing a sheepish, boyish grin. That alone made her heart patter oddly.

Mrs. Spenser smiled indulgently and then led the way from the parlor, up the stairs, and down a narrow hall to the back of the house. She opened the door to a large room and Birdie found herself in the most ornate bedchamber she had ever seen.

The large bed had a tasseled canopy and old-fashioned curtains in a pretty shade of robin's egg blue. Pale yellow touches and gilded prints decorated the walls. The entire room was elegant and peaceful.

More respite than bower of passion.

The lady crossed the room to a large dressing table, where a collection of pretty porcelain pots and an assortment of brushes and ribbons and gewgaws were scattered between half a dozen or so gilt-framed miniatures.

"My dear girl, go home. Now. Immediately. Before it is too late."

"Too late?" Even as Arabella said the words, she knew without a doubt that Mrs. Spenser was speaking from experience. She looked up and squarely at the woman.

"You may have him fooled, but I know who you are—"

Arabella opened her mouth to protest, but Mrs. Spenser staved her off with a short, crisp shake of her head. "That hair, those eyes. They are unmistakable, I would know a Tremont anywhere."

She shivered at the use of her real name and glanced over her shoulder to make sure Kingsley hadn't followed them. Still, she moved closer and whispered, "You won't tell—"

"Kingsley? Of course not. He's got his own secrets to keep," Mrs. Spenser replied with a dismissive flutter of her hand.

He did? Arabella's thoughts swam a little. As if she'd fallen in over her head.

Which of course she had.

"Please, Birdie," Mrs. Spenser implored. "Go home. Before you cannot go back. Beg your father's forgiveness over today's folly. Whatever has happened, I am certain Parkerton will forgive you."

"You know my father?" Arabella didn't know why, but this rather shocked her. Her uncle Jack was the rake of the family, certainly not her father . . . and yet . . .

"Don't be alarmed, my dear," Mrs. Spenser told her. "I've met any number of men in the *ton*. And I made the duke's acquaintance long before he met his dear wife. Not that he was my type. Far too stern for my taste."

Yes, the woman *had* met her father, Arabella realized.

"And while he is known for being rather hardheaded—"

That was an understatement.

"—you must go home and do your best to win his favor back."

There was a sense of finality to the woman's words that sent a chill down Arabella's spine. Still she couldn't help protesting, "Papa would never—"

"No, perhaps not, but once you've lost your heart, you won't have the resolve to do what must be done."

What must be done . . . Never mind the rest.

Still she couldn't help saying, "My heart?" Arabella shook her head. "It isn't . . . That is to say . . ." She turned her back to the lady so Mrs. Spenser couldn't see the truth in her lies.

She *was* falling in love with Kingsley.

The rattle of pots as Mrs. Spenser rearranged her dressing table pulled Arabella's attention back to the conversation at hand.

"You dear child," the lady began, "I've been in this business since before I was your age." She held out an open pot for Arabella. "What do you smell?"

"Roses," she began, for that was the first thing that tickled at her senses, but then something else wafted around her. "And—" She inhaled again, and now something else altogether different played with her senses.

Something deeper, something bewitching.

"Yes," Mrs. Spenser said, taking a sniff as well. "I love the layers of this perfume. The deeper one inhales, the more entwined one becomes."

Arabella glanced up at her and realized this was no longer about the perfume.

"It happens before you know it," Mrs. Spenser told her. "You think of only that first hint, that initial innocent and familiar air of roses, and then it becomes far more complex, and the layers wind around you, leaving you tangled in a web you cannot escape." She closed the pot and put it back on the table. "I know heartbreak when I see it . . ."

Heartbreak? Why, of all the nonsensical suggestions. Arabella considered herself far too sensible for that.

Yet, looming before her was a moment she was beginning to dread. With two tasks completed, all too soon the time would come when the major would set her down on the corner near her father's house and she would have to turn her back to him and walk away.

Her heart in shatters.

But what Mrs. Spenser said next added another layer, a far more complex one, to the entire caldron. " . . . and more's the pity, for that poor man is half-seas over in love with you."

Those words—*in love with you*—stopped Arabella cold. "With me?"

"Yes," Mrs. Spenser told her. "Not what you thought I was going to say, was it?"

She shook her head. "No. I hardly see how that could happen—"

"My dear girl, don't you read the gossip columns?" Mrs. Spenser asked.

"No, never!" Arabella told her. "Dreadful prattle. Lies and speculation, all of it." She shuddered for good measure.

"That's a pity," Mrs. Spenser said. "That also explains why—"

"Why what?"

"Oh, nothing," the lady replied in a breezy fashion. "And you are correct—there is hardly anything to be discovered in gossip."

But Arabella had the suspicion the lady didn't really believe what she was saying.

"Now, back to Major Kingsley and his poor heart—"

"Oh, you must be wrong, Mrs. Spenser. He cannot be . . ." For even if Kingsley did love her, it was all so impossible. And then the truth tumbled out. "He's to marry another."

"Is he now?" Mrs. Spenser, who had gone back to rearranging her dressing table, glanced over her shoulder, sounding only skeptical. "Then what is he doing with you?"

Giving me the day of my life, she wanted to say. And with it had come hints of a life full of adventure and, dare she desire it, passion, and something else she didn't dare hope for.

A word she didn't want to utter. Admit.

Especially now that she could see how the temptation of loving Kingsley might be her ruin.

Might? Make that *would*.

"It isn't possible." Arabella paused for a second. "Oh, if only it were." The words came out in a soft confession and a sheen of tears.

Mrs. Spenser folded her into her arms and gave her a hug. "Yes, I know, my dear girl. I know only too well."

"My father would kill him," she sniffled.

"There is that possibility," Mrs. Spenser agreed. "Or worse, something will change. Kingsley's opinions will change. And then . . ." Her words trailed off with a note of regret.

Arabella jerked back, dashing at the moisture in her eyes. "He wouldn't. He isn't like that."

"How do you know? You've only just met the man," the more experienced lady pointed out.

Shaking her head, Arabella dismissed it all as foolishness. "I daresay you haven't got the right of it. He's not in love with me—for it is as you say—too soon to fall in love."

But she didn't believe it, for she knew that her own heart had taken a terrible turn. And her desires. Oh, her desires for Kingsley . . .

They had her considering the impossible. How that kiss earlier shouldn't have ended. If he did love her . . .

She stopped herself right there.

Oh, bother! She needed to be sensible. But such a notion was so very much against everything inside her. Tremonts were reckless and willful. *Damn the consequences* should have been their motto.

For look how even her staid, dull father had become a very devil when he'd fallen in love with Elinor.

But if Kingsley loved her . . . Had fallen in love with her . . .

Visions of Paris and Venice and beyond danced in her imagination. Days of adventure. Nights of . . . Oh, yes, nights of passion that she had just tasted.

And if her father could be persuaded to let her follow her heart . . .

Impossible . . . Utterly impossible, she tried telling herself.

An opinion being echoed aloud by Mrs. Spenser. "Birdie, if you are gone too long . . . if things could become irreversible . . ."

"What do you mean by irreversible?" she asked, though she knew the answer to that. "That is to say, we haven't—"

Mrs. Spenser reached over and plucked at her hair, and then showed her the evidence: a small leaf from the hedge . . . The lady sighed and put it down on the tabletop beside a portrait. After a slight pause, she picked up the miniature, her finger running around the edge as if it had traced that path many times over.

"Go home," she said softly, firmly.

A chill ran along Arabella's spine as she looked not at the courtesan, but at the portrait of a small boy. Then her gaze swept over the table and she realized all the miniatures held the same image—at various ages—of this boy. As a bundled baby, a toddler in curls, and lastly as a handsome young adolescent.

A flicker of sadness crossed Mrs. Spenser's pretty features. The sort that spoke of a heartbreak that would never find healing.

This child, his child—whoever *he* was—had been everything to the lady, but no more.

Like the perfume in the jar, her heart had been stoppered away, hidden, lost.

With only a faint, fleeting moment captured in watercolor to remind her, to haunt her for the rest of her days.

Mrs. Spenser had made her choice. Once. Long ago.

And now it was Arabella's turn to make hers.

"There you go," Major Kingsley said, as he handed Arabella up into his waiting carriage.

She stole a glance at him as he strode around the carriage.

He couldn't be falling in love with her. The notion was ridiculous.

Impossible.

He went around to his side and climbed in, smiling at her with that wicked, boyish grin of his.

Oh, heavens, how her heart pattered. What if he was?

In an instant, Mrs. Spenser's warning rang anew. *You'll be unable to separate . . . Bound together . . . He'll refuse you nothing until. . .*

She shook her head, tossing out the horrible reckoning that would follow such a scenario.

Instead, she began to scold herself with a litany meant to rattle her back into a sensible state.

Kingsley wasn't in love with her. There it was.

He was far too sensible of a gentleman.

Yet would a sensible gentleman have agreed to her madcap scheme?

Certainly not.

Had the major been of a sensible nature, she most likely would never have met him. He wouldn't have come seeking her company at the Setchfield ball, mistaken identity or not.

More to the point, he wouldn't have even attended such a scandal-ridden event. Not ever.

She shivered and drew her pelisse tighter around her shoulders.

Nor would he have kissed her earlier if he were the sensible sort. For it had hardly been a proper sort of kiss.

He'd kissed her hungrily . . . Like he'd never desired any woman more than he had her. . .

Oh, good heavens! Mrs. Spenser might be right.

Arabella peeked out from beneath the brim of her bonnet. She hadn't realized it before now, but she'd been hiding beneath it, rolled up into a tight knot of alarm.

Kingsley in love with her? That would never do. As she'd told Mrs. Spenser, it was impossible.

Perfectly impossible for them to be in love. And she knew it right down to her toes. Just as she knew what needed to be done.

Kingsley caught her looking over at him and grinned again. That charming air stopped her heart, left her enchanted.

If she inhaled right now, she knew she'd wake up from this dreamy state as entwined, as captivated as if he'd bound her in chains.

And yet, here he was asking her the one question that

would reveal everything. If he was willing to refuse her nothing, then . . .

"So what is it to be, my little Birdie? Home or one last adventure?"

So she told him.

CHAPTER 9

Kingsley turned and gaped at the lady beside him. Surely he hadn't heard her correctly. "You want to do what?"

"You heard me perfectly well," Birdie told him, nose tipping in the air with an imperious tilt. "I want to break into a house."

"You want to take up a life of crime?"

"Haven't you ever wanted to?"

"No!" An answer to her question and her outlandish request.

Housebreaking, indeed! Whatever would she suggest next?

Make love to me, Kingsley, came an irreverent thought.

No, no! Not that, he realized with a bit of panic. He might be able to refuse her larcenous inclinations, but the other?

He didn't think he had the will to say what needed to be said.

No. Never. Absolutely not.

But oh, the devil take him, Augie's bullet or not, he wanted her.

Meanwhile, she'd crossed her arms over her chest and had

made a matronly and defiant *harrumph* over his refusal. "And here I thought you were an adventurous sort."

Something about her words pricked at his pride ever so slightly, but it was enough to get him to rise to her bait—even against his better judgment. "I'll have you know there is *adventure* and then there is *crime*. And crime, such as you are suggesting, my pretty little filching mort, will see you standing in the Old Bailey being consigned to a hanging."

"Then I daresay it would be best if we weren't caught."

"Not caught!" He shook his head. "At least now I know where you live."

"However do you know that?"

"Because I'm quite certain the place you escaped from earlier was Bedlam."

"Bedlam, indeed," she sniffed.

"Whyever would you want to break into someone's house?"

She shrugged. "I just merely want to try. It can't be that difficult. Thieves do it all the time."

"And are hung all the time."

"You are quite preoccupied with the state of your neck."

"I rather like my neck," he told her. "And I must confess, I'm a bit alarmed by the fact that it seems you've spent a considerable amount of time planning this ridiculous scheme."

"I have," she admitted rather proudly. "When one isn't allowed any sort of freedom, one has plenty of time to imagine all sorts of things."

"Larceny and petty crime are hardly suitable subjects to be pondering."

"You sound as stuffy as my father," she declared. "Besides,

having given this considerable thought—as you were so kind to point out—it is more than obvious, I have no intention of being caught. I've considered all the difficulties and know exactly how it ought to be done properly."

"Properly?" he scoffed. "Have you ever met a criminal?"

Her mouth opened and she looked to be about to declare that she had, but then her mouth closed as if, under a bit of consideration, she thought better of answering.

"Suffice it to say, I have every confidence in my plan," she finally said. "We need only find an empty house."

Oh, was that all?

"In the middle of the Season?"

"There are several that are empty now," she replied. "Why, there are at least half a dozen house parties over the next fortnight and they've all but emptied the *ton*—a number of which have very large houses."

"How do you know—?"

"Major Kingsley, everyone knows. Especially if one isn't invited," she told him, glancing away. "Or is."

There was some truth in that. Why, his mother's house party was responsible for a good half a dozen or more vacancies.

"Now I've told you my third and final request," Birdie continued, "and if you don't mind, I would like to be about it as quickly as possible."

She made it sound like all she wanted him to do was track down the right shade of green thread. Or fetch some new candles from the shop across the way.

Oh, of all the madness! Breaking into empty houses.

Kingsley paused as a madcap idea—as ridiculous as her request—came to him. *An empty house.*

Oh, good God. He didn't dare. Then again . . .

He had to press his lips together not to laugh.

"I might know of a house," he managed, trying his best to sound helpful.

Her glance was nothing but suspicion.

"I have it on good authority the owner has gone to a house party—just as you suggested."

"Some bachelor residence?" She shook her head. "No, no, that will never do. It has to be a house of some size, significance."

"I think you will find this house exactly to your liking."

Her gaze narrowed.

"Have I disappointed you yet, minx?"

Her admission took a while to come out. "No."

Grinning, he turned the horses toward Mayfair.

"If we are going to do this, you must do exactly as I say," Kingsley began.

"Oh, not this again," Birdie complained as they stood in the shadows of the mews behind a house just off Grosvenor Square. Dusk had finally come upon them and now night was drawing a thick curtain over London. Here and there candles were being lit and the street lighters were making their rounds. But here, behind a large house, the alleyway was all shadows. "I doubt me being a Flemish housebreaker is going to save my neck if we get nicked."

He turned and faced her. "If we get 'nicked.' Listen to you. Next you'll be telling me your family is full of smugglers and spies."

An odd look passed over her face, but then she laughed a little and shrugged his suggestion off. "Listen to me? Listen to you! Smugglers, indeed." She glanced away as she finished, "Of all the ridiculous notions."

"Still, you'll do exactly as I say," he continued. "Or else I will cart you back to the carriage and deposit you in the middle of Seven Dials . . . Where I am inclined to believe you most likely belong."

"Of all the insulting—" She began to move past him toward the gate, but he caught her by the arm and pulled her up short.

"My way or else," he told her.

"This is my plan," she continued, doggedly refusing to give in.

"Your plan, but I would remind you it is my neck you are risking." He took a furtive glance up and down the dark mews. *And his reputation . . . And his familial relations . . .*

"My neck as well," she pointed out.

"And a pretty one it is. I would prefer not to see it stretched."

"No wonder you don't have a mistress," she whispered. "That was a terrible compliment."

"It wasn't intended as one. When I compliment you, you'll know it." He edged up to the gate and opened the door. "Now, no more arguments. Agreed?"

She nodded.

"Good. I shall go first, and you will do exactly as I say."

"If I must," she muttered as he slid silently into the shadowed yard beyond.

"You must," he shot over his shoulder.

"Tyrant."

"I heard that," he replied as he made his way along the wall to the side of the house.

She followed, and to her credit, quietly and without any further arguments. It was almost as if stealth and thievery were in her blood.

When they got to a window, he paused, studying the frames that ran on either side and the ones above them—all of which were dark.

"No one appears to be home," she said, albeit a bit begrudgingly.

"No one is," he told her, as he ever so slowly began opening the window before them.

"However did you know—?"

As he pushed it open the rest of the way, he explained, "I noticed the window wasn't barred a few nights ago during a supper party."

"You know the owner?" she asked, trying not to sound overly scandalized.

"You might say that," he admitted, as he hoisted himself up and through the now open window. Then he leaned over the sill and offered her his hand.

Her fingers wound around his—she was such a contradiction in so many ways, but the strength in her hands spoke of a fortitude behind her impulsive, madcap notions—and he pulled her up and in.

Of course she landed right in his arms, tumbling into his grasp like a whirlwind.

How was it Birdie always ended up so? In his arms . . . Up against him . . .

Where she belongs, Fate seemed to whisper in his ear.

Damn Mrs. Spenser and her confounding assurances of Fate.

Birdie took her time finding her footing, one hand clinging to the sleeve of his coat, the other shaking out her skirt. Every time she rustled against him, his body seemed to grow tighter.

This demmed clamoring need to have her was waking up and making unreasonable demands.

The house is empty, after all.

Kingsley gulped for a bit of air.

"Hardly seems like much of a break-in when you know the owner," she was saying, "knew the window was unlocked, and have it on good authority that no one is home."

Yes, well, there was that. He had rather hoped she'd just be satisfied getting into the house and having a bit of a look around and wouldn't start putting that sharp and inquisitive mind of hers to work.

"Excellent planning is what I call it," he told her. Better that than the truth.

He had no doubts there would be the devil to pay if she realized whose house she'd just broken into.

Oh, yes, he could very well imagine the choice words she'd have for his deception.

Right now he had a few words of his own—for having her in his arms was working its own dangerous witchery on his senses, and he couldn't help himself as he brushed a stray strand of her hair off her cheek, carefully tucking it back up into the loose knot at the back of her neck.

She stilled as his fingers traced a lazy trail down the line of her jaw; he paused there and let his finger curl under her chin, tipping it up and dipping his head down to take the one thing he wanted more than anything.

Her.

Arabella dodged Kingsley's seductive attempt, slipping from his arms. For a moment, she'd stood there mesmerized, like a sleeping princess awaiting a knight's kiss to awaken her, but Mrs. Spenser's haunting warning was what prodded her to step away.

. . . once you've lost your heart, you won't have the resolve to do what must be done.

She just wouldn't let it come to that. Truly, it was that simple.

"If the house is empty," she began, hoping her voice didn't tremble in the same uneven way her heart was pattering, "then perhaps we should take a look around before we leave."

"You want a tour?" He needn't sound so incredulous. "That is all you meant to do once you got in here? Look around like a country tourist?"

"Hardly," she replied, because, in all honesty, she truly hadn't thought much beyond just getting in. "But I have no need for someone else's silver or jewels. Or whatever it is thieves take."

"Then what do you want, my mysterious little minx," he said in a deep, husky voice that purred down her spine. Every note, every word teased her to confess.

What do you want?

Arabella laid her hand on the edge of the grand table and steadied herself. Holland cloths covered everything else in the room, hiding them away from prying eyes.

What do you want? The question prodded at her.

For what she really, truly wanted was impossible.

Wasn't it?

"As I said, we aren't here to commit any crimes," she pointed out. "I merely asked you to help me break in."

Kingsley laughed at her. "Some thief you make. And I would note, breaking in is a crime."

"I suppose it might be viewed that way," she admitted, realizing now the utter folly of her request. For here they were, in what appeared to be an elegantly appointed house, all alone.

Alone.

Oh, that was folly indeed. Dangerous and reckless.

Arabella panicked a bit. "Well, if we aren't going to take a tour, I suppose there is nothing left to do but have you return me home." She turned back toward the open window. The one that led to a much safer place.

A cold, dark alleyway.

Behind her, Kingsley's reply was a tempting whisper. "If that really is what you want."

It wasn't. The realization hit her so hard, she was glad she was still close enough to the table to reach for it. For once the major returned her, she'd never see him again. He'd drive away, turn a corner, and be nothing more than a memory.

Like the fading notes of Mrs. Spenser's rare perfume. There, and then gone.

Suddenly Arabella knew exactly what the lady had been telling her. Warning her.

The deeper one inhales, the more one is entwined. Caught. Trapped.

"You do realize the house is empty," he was saying as he came a bit closer. "Ours for as long as we want."

"*Want?*" Oh, bother! There was that word again. Arabella tried to breathe. Tried to tell herself, convince herself, she wanted for nothing.

Yet that was no longer the case. She'd spent the entire day with Kingsley, brushing up against him in the narrow seat of the curricle, strolling about the field at the match, her fingers curled into the curve of his muscled arm, and then there had been the bower . . .

No. She mustn't think about the bower, his kiss . . .

But how could she not when it had awakened her to something as rare as that bewitching concoction in that bejeweled pot.

Her gaze flew up to meet Kingsley's. His dark, moody eyes pulled her deeper into a dangerous abyss. "I think a tour wouldn't be amiss. We've come this far, haven't we?"

"Adding to the terms of our agreement?" he teased, stalking around the table.

This time she didn't flee. "I suppose I am." She tipped her chin up, defiantly. And perhaps, offering.

He grinned and took her hand, his fingers warm around hers. How was it that when they touched, when he held her, she felt nothing but wonder?

"I'll make an exception this time," he told her, leading her from the dining room. "But don't get any ideas that you can start renegotiating the rest of our agreement."

"I would hardly—"

"Yes, you would," he said, laughing. "Now come along, my almost-thief, and I will show you the house you propose not to rob."

"What if I change my idea and decide I want to steal something?"

"I'm counting on it," he teased as they entered a grand foyer.

She looked around the oval entryway. Outside, a gaslight illuminated the street; the soft glow stole inside, shining a narrow path for them. "I don't recall you saying whose house this was."

"I didn't," he replied as he walked over to the footman's closet by the door and took out a flint. He struck a light to one of the candles. He held the light aloft and she could see the foyer rose all the way up to the roof, the stairs winding around in a dizzy circle. "I doubt you would have been here, for it has been leased for years by a disagreeable old fellow." He led her to the stairs. "The owner only recently took up residence."

"But you seem to know . . ."

He paused for a moment. "I've stayed here before. When I've come to London."

"Oh," she murmured, glancing at the paintings lining the walls that rose above, but found no clues—only unfamiliar faces. Handsome devils, much like Kingsley, with strong features and a rakish gleam to their eyes, but nothing that gave her any indication as to who the mysterious owner might be.

Yet Kingsley knew. Was on such intimate terms with the family that he stayed with them.

She glanced again at the row of portraits and wished she could rattle the answers out of one of them—for certainly the man leading the way couldn't be counted upon to be very forthcoming.

Then again, neither was she.

Well, there was that, she conceded.

They had climbed the stairs to the first floor and came to a small room in the back. Kingsley strolled in and glanced around, then made his way to a cabinet not far from the fireplace. He opened it and pulled out a bottle. "A toast to the end of our adventures?"

Arabella shook her head. The last thing she needed were spirits clouding her judgment.

Nor did she want the adventures to end.

But they must, she told herself. *They must.*

Kingsley, meanwhile, had merely shrugged and poured himself a measure.

"I see you aren't opposed to stealing," she remarked, prowling about the room. She didn't know what she was looking for, but hoped to find something that might point her in the right direction.

Help her choose her path at the crossroads she was certain now loomed before her.

"Stealing? Hardly. It is just a drink." He chuckled. "Nothing more than any good host would offer." He winked at her and then tossed back his purloined brandy.

"Wicked devil," she scolded as she looked over the shelves—a mixture of books—travelogues, histories, tomes on philosophy, and a spattering of novels. Even a few volumes of poetry. Mixed in were the usual vases and small statues that suggested the owner was someone who knew how to balance beauty and art. "But I see why you are friends with our mysterious host."

"How is that?"

"He shares your love of travel and art."

"How do you know the owner is a man? Might a woman live here?"

A woman? A flare of jealousy unlike anything she'd ever known rattled through her. Yet once she glanced around the very masculine room, those dreadful green notes abated quickly. "Hardly. If this house belongs to a woman, then this room is missing a pianoforte and a settee by the window."

He looked around and smiled slowly. "Is that what you would add?"

"Not the pianoforte—I cannot play a note. But I would put a better chair by that window." She pointed to the one in the back of the room. "It seems an excellent spot for reading. And I'm correct, aren't I? There isn't a woman here."

They both knew what she was asking.

"No. There isn't a woman. Just another crabbed old bachelor."

"Truly?" Arabella paused, a French volume catching her eye. She almost smiled for she knew the small, narrow book well. That tome, whose title, loosely translated read *The School of Venus*, had been a scandalous forbidden treasure at Miss Emery's. Brought to those proper and hallowed halls by none other than Thalia Langley, the wild, headstrong daughter of the very notorious Lord Langley.

Thalia's copy had been passed around in the dark of night until it had become dog-eared and worn.

Of course, Arabella had read it. Twice.

Glancing over her shoulder, she looked the major up and down, and wondered if he had ever read it. Ever done any of the beguiling acts described there in such . . . detail.

Details that now came back to Arabella, leaving her wondering what it would be like to take him, that very manly part of him, in her hand and watch him . . .

Oh, what had the book said? Ah, yes. *Grow. Harden. Take root.*

She pressed her lips together and hoped her cheeks weren't flaming with mortification.

"Whatever have you found over there?" he asked, coming to her side.

Arabella tried to move in front of the book, so he wouldn't see what had gained her attention, but it was too late.

"Your crabbed bachelor has an eye for French fiction," she said, moving away as Kingsley plucked the book from the shelf.

He looked up from the title and grinned at her.

Suddenly the room seemed all too small, all too confining and she backed out into the shadows of the hall. She considered her choices, and something about the door across the way beckoned her.

And so she opened it.

"That book is definitely not fiction," he was saying as he followed her out into the hall.

Arabella, who had been surveying the room before her, turned and looked at the major. Saw him as she imagined she would never see him again. As unexplored. A mystery.

Her heart's desire.

For she'd opened a door she had no wish to close.

Birdie stood silhouetted in the doorway, and the only other thing he could see in the shadows beyond was a large bed.

His bed, to be exact.

Which wasn't much of a surprise since this was his house.

He hadn't lied to her when he said he'd stayed here a time or two, or that he'd been at a supper party the other night.

And truth of it had weighed on him as she'd followed up the stairs, chattering away about the paintings, tossing questions at him in hopes of discovering something about him.

All the while, he hadn't been able to stop wondering what it would be like to hear her voice every day, across the dining table, calling for him when he came home, or in the morning, as the first bit of light came crawling into his bedchamber.

Her voice, her eyes, her touch, lighting his day. Every day.

It was a notion that sent his blood racing. Left him cold with fear.

Impossible, his better senses raged.

His parents had higher plans for him, a much loftier bride than some chit in a milkmaid costume who'd caught his eye at the Setchfield ball—*the Setchfield ball, of all places,* he could hear his father casting back at him with nothing but disdain.

Nor would the fact that he'd plucked her from the streets like a waif do anything to win his parents' approval.

Yet his heart, oh, bother his heart. It sang a different song. Pushed across the narrow gulf of a hallway that separated them by a need he could no longer resist, he caught Birdie in his arms and carried her toward his bed.

CHAPTER 10

The air left Arabella's lungs even as her feet rose from the floor, swept as she was into Kingsley's arms.

Not that she would have protested. Not when his lips caught hers and he kissed her—hard and swift. His tongue teasing, prompting, demanding entrance, and willingly, she opened herself to him.

She'd had only a second to survey her surroundings before he'd taken hold of her—the chamber half hidden beneath Holland covers and the bed made up and ready for the next occupant.

"Whose room is this?" she managed to ask when Kingsley's lips moved from hers to explore the nape of her neck.

She didn't know why, but it mattered.

"Mine," he said, taking much the same sort of furtive glance about as she had. "The room is mine."

"Yours? But I thought—"

He pulled back a bit, one hand cradling her chin. "I told you, minx. I have use of the house. I slept here just last night, if you must know."

Just last night.

Her gaze flitted to the large bed behind her. The rich coverlet that offered warmth. The wide, deep mattress.

Then she looked back at him.

From the light in his eyes, the hunger in his kiss, Arabella knew sleeping was the furthest thing from Kingsley's mind.

He leaned in and kissed her, this time gently, coaxing her to join him.

Join him in his bed.

Yet warnings clamored from what seemed like another lifetime. From far away.

If things become irreversible. . .

But things already were, Arabella realized. She'd never be able to walk away from Kingsley—not without knowing . . . this.

However would she live the rest of her days wondering what might have happened?

Not when she knew what she wanted.

She wanted him to touch her as he had at the Setchfield ball. She wanted him to devour her as he'd promised that night. She wanted to feel as she had in the bower—her body thrumming alive, and Kingsley hard against her.

As he was right now.

"Birdie, I—"

She stopped him with a kiss of her own, rising up on her tiptoes, bringing her body up against his, her hips undulating against his groin, against *him*.

That, that long hard length of him, straining against the front of his breeches, left her shivering. Longing, as the book of Venus had promised, for him to fill her, stroke her, tease her until . . .

Oh, until. . .

That was the temptation that called to her.

Until. . .

That single word held a clarion note she couldn't resist.

"I want—" he whispered in her ear, as his hand curled under her breast, his thumb rubbing at her nipple. His other hand cupped her bottom and pulled her close, so she rode up and down against him.

Her mouth opened and he kissed her—it was a moment of such deep need—his tongue tracing over hers, his fingers bringing her nipple to a sensitive point, and her very core, that private place—private no more as it seemed to find a way to come alive each time her hips swayed toward him.

Want. Yes, she wanted him as well.

And the devil knew it, for his hand caught hold of her skirt and pulled it up, his fingers sliding right to that quivering, aching spot.

At first she panicked a bit—she'd never been touched so, but he grinned at her, and kissed her again, kissed her deeply, until a soft, anxious mew of pleasure slipped from her, and then he touched her yet again.

This time, Arabella's legs opened to him, just as her lips had, welcoming him, and he began to tease her open.

When he slid over her, she gasped as he found the perfect spot.

And just as he'd promised a sennight earlier at the ball, he began to devour her.

She gasped for air as his fingers teased her, round and round he circled her, sliding his finger inside her, until she was wet and trembling—barely able to remember her name.

Oh, but she knew his.

"Kingsley," she gasped, even as he pulled his hand away and shrugged off his coat.

She reached for him, teetering and lost without him holding her.

Catching hold of his waistcoat, she focused on the solid masculine, and worst of all, still clad wall before her. Oh, that would never do—him with his clothes on.

A madness came over her.

And so she plucked the buttons before her open, pulling his waistcoat free, then tugging his shirt from his breeches and pulling it up and over his head until he was bare-chested before her.

Arabella drew a steadying breath, for while she'd seen men stripped to their waists before, she hadn't seen anything quite like Kingsley.

He was so very masculine—proportioned like one of Elgin's marbles—with broad, strong planes and hard lines. He was just so very hard—and yet when he held her, when he touched her, she felt something quite opposite.

A dangerous gentleness capable of coaxing her, leading her down a tempting path.

Oh, and she was so very tempted. Filled with desire.

She hadn't even noticed that while he'd been touching her, bringing her close, he'd also managed to undo the buttons down the back of her gown.

"You're much better at that," she teased as her gown fell to the floor.

"I prefer the undoing part." Apparently with good reason. His head dipped down and his lips caught hold of her nipple. This time it was his tongue that teased her, suckling her, and again she was tossed into a tempest.

"Ah, yes, the undoing is the best part," he told her as he moved to her other breast, working the same wet, hot magic on that side.

Ah, yes. Undone was best, Arabella wanted to tell him, as his hands, his lips explored her.

And then she knew he was gaining an advantage.

"Let me see how this undoing works," she whispered, reaching out and slipping the first button free from his breeches, the back of her hand sliding over him.

All the way down.

He stilled, his mouth opening to say something, yet no words came out, his dark gaze locked on hers. Then he grinned, ever so slightly, as if to dare her to do it again.

And so she did.

The second button opened and then the third, and she watched his face, his gaze narrow as his world teased into just that—her touch, her hold on him.

Oh, yes, so this undoing could work both ways, and in that knowledge, Arabella came into her own. That boldness that made her a Tremont sang through her blood.

Beneath her fingers, his breeches strained, and when she undid the final button, slowly, deliberately, using both hands and taking advantage of his captivity to tease him terribly, suddenly he was free, and she caught hold of him, marveling at his length, the feel of him.

Silken smooth. And hard. And throbbing, much as she was.

She didn't realize it, but she'd been holding her breath, waiting for this. When she could hold him, tease him as he'd done her. Running her hand down him and then back up, marveling as he threw back his head and made a noise that was both a growl and triumphant.

Her thumb rolled over the round full tip, a bead of moisture welling up, and she used it to slide over him, her touch now slick and hot.

As she stroked him, what she hadn't expected was how it would tease her. He was holding her close, whispering in her ear, and leaving a trail of hot eager kisses on the nape of her neck, yet all she could think of was the ache between her legs.

The ache only he could ease.

"Kingsley, I want—" Her lashes fluttered as the words failed her. "Please," she finally managed.

She didn't need to ask again. He eased her back onto the bed, grinning as she sank into the mattress.

And when he followed, climbing atop her, she opened herself to him.

Yet as she curled up and into his embrace, she sensed a hesitation about him.

Having spent the last sennight imagining just this, Kingsley naked, over her, filling her, Arabella wasn't willing to wait any longer.

"Kingsley," she whispered. "You promised."

Kingsley looked down at the beauty in his bed and had only one thought, to make her his.

Forever.

His tempestuous, beautiful, willful Birdie. His always.

As he climbed in, covering her body with his, he knew he'd never been so hard, so full of need.

Her touch had been so innocent to begin with, but it hadn't taken her long to become bold.

Bold was one thing, but innocent?

Good God, what the hell was he doing?

He was about to climb out of the bed, but her hand curved around his cheek.

"Kingsley, you promised." She smiled up at him, a sensuous, tempting curve to her lips.

Yes, he had. But not like she thought. The promise he was making as his hand caught hold of her rounded bottom, and lifted her to him, was the sort he'd explain in the morning.

The rest of their lives, but right now even as her legs opened to him, one curling around his hip, he knew only one thing.

Birdie.

She stretched and coiled to be closer to him, and he eased himself into her tight, hot channel.

"This might hurt," he told her as he entered her. "But only for a moment." And then he kissed her again, deeply, thoroughly as he had before, until she was once again writhing against him, mewing with pleasure, and it was then he pushed past the barrier he'd met and made her his.

Hurt? Arabella had barely registered the word as Kingsley's lips once again claimed her. His kiss, still tasting of the brandy he'd had in the other room, was as intoxicating as the liquor itself. His tongue teasing her much as she realized he would tease her with his manhood, for she could feel him beginning to fill her, her body opening to him, stretching.

It was nearly too much for her, but then he was inside her, with a thrust that broke past her innocence.

For a moment, Arabella found herself wrenched back into the world, but Kingsley caught hold of her, easing in and out of her, kissing her, teasing her, thrusting again, and this time, there was no pain.

Far from it.

Those tendrils, born of his touch, his kiss, uncoiled within her, drawing her closer to him.

He continued to fill her, whispering words meant only for her, his kiss growing more hungry, more urgent, and she knew why—for she felt the same haphazard pull upward.

She followed, her fingers clinging to his shoulders, holding on to him, and when he gave one hard, frantic thrust, gasping out her name, "Birdie!" she found herself wrested along with him, a wicked, magical wave leading her to her release. It was as if all the coils and tangles that had bound them together suddenly let go and she was adrift with him, languid and free all at once.

"Oh, yes," she agreed. "Yes, Kingsley."

And he rolled to one side, bringing her with him, and they held each other as the unruly waves continued to toss them, safe in each other's arms.

Arabella found herself nestled in a warm cocoon when she awoke sometime later. It wasn't the strange place, or the fact that she was curled up next to an entirely naked man that startled her—on the contrary, the naked man part made her suddenly restless and . . . hungry.

But there was something else that brought her back to her surroundings.

A softly whistled tune, a sweet romantic song that had called her from her sultry dreams.

She rolled toward the source, and even in the meager light, she could see the amusement on Kingsley's face as he continued to call to her, luring her awake.

"Teach me," she said, her fingers softly tracing the O his lips were making.

"Full of demands, aren't you, minx?"

"I am," she told him, cocking her head slightly.

"Changing the terms of our agreement yet again?"

"I am," she told him. "I haven't heard any complaints as to my last amendment."

"And you never will," he laughed, curling her back into his embrace.

"Teach me to whistle," she repeated.

"As you wish. Purse up your lips like this—" His lips puckered up and she followed suit.

But he just stared at her.

"Well? Am I doing it wrong?" she asked.

"No, but it's hard to remember what we were doing with your lips all ripe for kissing."

She swatted him on the shoulder.

Then she remembered.

If you must know, I was shot in the shoulder.

She scrambled to sit up. "Oh, heavens! I am so sorry. Is that where you were injured?"

He shook his head. "No. The other side. But I might note that you have the right hook of a French bullet."

While he reached up to rub the spot she'd contacted, Arabella's gaze flew to the other shoulder, her fingers following until they came to the puckered scars.

"It's all done and healed, sweetling," he told her. "I was lucky."

"I suppose," she said. "It must have been—"

"It was war. And it's well and over," he told her. "Though now I face my greatest challenge."

She sat back. "What is that?"

"Teaching you to whistle."

Now it was her turn to laugh.

"Just pucker your lips like this—"

Arabella did as he instructed.

"And put your tongue up on the roof of your mouth and blow."

She did as he said, but all that came out was a wet, sputtering noise that hardly resembled the sweet notes that had called her awake.

Kingsley laughed at her attempt—that is, after he wiped his now damp face.

"What is so funny?" she demanded, pursing her lips again and forcing a sound out that in no way resembled the merry tune the milkmaid made so effortlessly.

"You," he told her as his hand curled around her chin and raised it up so she was looking right at him.

"Me?"

"Yes," he said quietly as his head dipped down. "You are a bird with no song."

I was until today, she thought as his lips covered hers yet again, and their bodies fit back together, finding the rhythm that sang a song only they could hear.

W hen Arabella awoke, the sun was starting to peek over the roofs and ridgelines of London. With it being so late in the spring, nearly summer, she knew the hour was early. Far earlier than she usually got up.

Today, she realized, smiling at the bright hint of sunshine, she was akin to the milkmaid.

And her smile only widened as she rolled over looking for Kingsley. But her joy was short-lived, for to her shock she found herself alone, the space beside her cold.

He was gone.

"Not gone," she told herself, as she scuttled out of the great bed, only to find her body was tender and shaky all at once—unused as it was to spending a night making love.

He did love her. *He did.*

Once she found her footing, she fished around for her clothes, scattered as they were over the Turkish carpet.

Kingsley's, she noted, were gone.

"Not to worry," she told herself as she hurriedly dressed. "He's close at hand."

But he wasn't. The library across the hall was empty. As was the rest of the floor. She hurried down the stairs, past the paintings, which the night before had seemed rakish and devil-may-care.

Now they all frowned down at her in scornful disdain.

"He is here," she told an imperious-looking matron hung over the last stair.

Yet he wasn't. The house was empty. She called for him, and then searched the main floor, even venturing down into the kitchen, which was cold and dark.

As she returned to the foyer by the front door, her heart raced.

He's here, it seemed to be saying. *He must be.*

Yet when she got to the dining room, she spied the window they'd come in through, cracked open.

She went to the sill and hoisted the frame open the rest of the way, but there was no sign of him in the gardens beyond.

Kingsley was gone. Well and gone.

Arabella's legs gave out beneath her as the realization hit her full force; an echo of Mrs. Spenser's warning rang through her.

Or worse, something will change. Kingsley's opinions will change. And then. . .

Everything had changed and now . . . he'd abandoned her.

No, no, it cannot be, her heart cried out. *You're mistaken.*

Her fingers curled into the heavy frame and she laid her forehead against the smooth wood. Willed the tears rising in her eyes to remain where they belonged, shuttered tight inside her heart.

Yet they escaped, despite her best intentions, and the sobs that followed came in great, gulping moans.

For as only a Tremont would know, when one gambled, when one put all their cards on the table, it was just as likely that they would lose.

And Arabella had done just that, wagered everything she had on last night, and lost it all come morning.

Including her heart.

Sitting down on the hard parquet floor, she swiped at her nose with the back of her sleeve.

Oh, good heavens, whatever was she supposed to do now? She wasn't even too sure where in London she was, or how to get home. There was no footman to send for a carriage. No one to take a note to her father to come and fetch her.

She glanced down at herself and realized she was a rumpled mess.

Not even dear Cantley would recognize her if she even managed to find her own front door.

Home. She took another tremulous glance down at her state of *dishabille* and wondered if her father would even let her in.

If. . .

That *if* relied on the very unlikely hope of finding her way home.

Yet rescue came not like a knight on a horse, spurs jangling and horse snorting and pawing at the ground, but in the clank of a wagon and the bright notes of a jaunty whistle.

Arabella sat up, for the song was not unlike the one Kingsley had tried to teach her the night before. She sniffed one more time and then absently swiped at her nose and remaining tears.

Getting up, she poked her head out the opening and looked toward the mews.

Again that song sent a tingle down her spine, called to her even as she heard the clank of buckets that signaled not her knight errant, or rather her errant knight, but someone else.

Next door the garden gate swung open, and over the wall, Arabella spied a milkmaid dashing up the walk toward the kitchen door.

The milkmaid! Her milkmaid.

She all but launched herself out the window, tumbling over the window frame and falling onto the grass below.

"Botheration," she cursed as she righted herself, for now there was a large green stain down the front of her muslin gown.

No matter. She'd be home in no time.

She hurried out the garden gate and came nearly nose to nose with the girl she'd envied all these months.

Close up, the milkmaid had mousy brown hair and a stub of a nose, while her cheeks were bright like a bushel of fall apples. A dark spattering of freckles covered her face.

"Gar!" the girl said, stepping back. "You demmed well scared me witless! I've a good mind to—" She raised her bucket and looked to be about to dash it over Arabella's head, when she stopped, her bucket held aloft while her mouth fell open. "Gar! I'm going bloody mad." She closed her eyes and shook her head, but when she opened her stubby dark lashes again, she looked at Arabella like she was seeing a ghost.

Which in some sense, she was.

"You know who I am, don't you?" Arabella asked.

The girl nodded, and slowly the bucket came down to rest beside her hip.

"And you know where my house is, don't you?"

"Aye," the girl replied as if testing the word.

"Can you take me there?"

The girl tipped her head and studied Arabella from the top of her tousled hair to the rumpled state of her hem. "Gotten lost, have ya?"

"Yes, I fear so," Arabella admitted.

"Then you best be getting in beside me. London is no place for a lady."

"So I've been told." She followed the girl to the back of the wagon, where the milkmaid hopped up and in with a practiced ease. When she looked back and could see the hesitation in Arabella's stance, she held out her hand and pulled her up.

When she smiled, Arabella could see her teeth were crooked, but there was a kindness in her eyes that confirmed everything Arabella had ever suspected about her.

Then the milkmaid glanced over her shoulder, where the old man who drove the wagon gaped at the pair of them. "Oh, gar, close your mouth there, ol' Pete, afore you catch flies. She isn't the first girl to come home like this." The girl turned around and winked at Arabella, her legs swinging over the end of the wagon. "And I feared you won't be the last."

The wagon lurched to a start, and Arabella had to catch hold of the railing to keep from tumbling out.

Down the alleyway they went, stopping for the girl to deliver the milk, her jaunty whistle heralding in the day, just as dependable as the sun.

CHAPTER 11

The Duke of Parkerton was at his wit's end.

"We'll find her," his brother Jack promised for about the hundredth time. But even now, Jack's notorious rakish confidence seemed to be waning. "We'll find her," he repeated, this time, it seemed, for himself.

"How?" Parkerton asked, looking up and down the traffic-clogged streets. They'd searched for Arabella all the day before and through the night and now, without a lick of sleep, the duke was even more determined to find where his missing daughter had gone.

"By not giving up," Jack replied. He turned and tipped his hat in promise to Elinor, and again to his wife, Miranda, who stood arm in arm with the duchess.

Parkerton ruffled at the very thought. Give up? *Never.* He'd forgive his daughter anything to have her back. She could take the rest of her life to find a husband if she so desired.

Just so she came home.

Arabella. His dear and beautiful daughter. His heart

clenched tight in his chest and he wished for the thousandth time he could just summon her home.

Then as he swung up into his saddle, he heard the sunny whistle of the milkmaid coming down the street. The bright, merry refrain stopped him cold for it was the very same tune that Arabella had held out as the clarion call of freedom.

If only he'd listened to her then. Let her follow her heart.

What was it Elinor had said about holding her so tight? *She'd slip away eventually.*

And she had.

"Parkerton," Jack said, nudging him, and nodding toward the milk wagon.

Sitting alongside the milkmaid was a bedraggled but familiar figure.

"Arabella!" Parkerton exclaimed, leaping from his horse and crossing the distance between them in a flash.

"Papa!" Arabella said, rushing to him. "I'm so sorry."

"No, no, I was wrong," he told her as he enfolded her into his arms.

Oh, good God! She was home. Relief flooded him as he held her out at arm's length and gave her a sweeping examination.

That was until she spoke.

"I'll go to Landsdowne," she said, agony biting at her words. "Take me today. I'll marry whoever you wish. Just take me far from London."

Kingsley had searched high and low for Birdie most of the morning, driving circles through Mayfair, hoping to catch sight of her blue bonnet or even a ringlet of chestnut hair.

He'd left the house for only a short time—having gone out to find them something to break their fast, because he had grand plans for the day.

Yet by the time he'd returned, his Birdie had taken flight.

But his search was to no avail, until he was riding round Berkeley Square—yet again—when he spied someone he did know.

"Augie," he called out, pulling his horses to a stop.

His friend nearly jumped out of his jacket. "What the devil! Kingsley! Don't sneak up on a fellow like that. Poorly done, my good man. Poorly done." Lord Augustus tugged at his jacket, while his jaw worked back and forth.

"I need your assistance. You've got to help me find her," Kingsley said, his hand raking through his hair.

"Find who?" Augie asked.

Find who? He needed to ask? Kingsley thought he was going mad. "Birdie. I've got to find Birdie."

Augie's eyes widened and then turned murderous. "You lost her?"

"No. Well, sort of—"

"Good God, man, what have you done?"

Kingsley groaned. "She ran away from me. I need to find her. Please, Augie, you must help me."

"Don't see why I should help you if Birdie felt the need to run away," he huffed, and turned to leave.

"I want to make her my wife," he all but shouted at Augie's departing back.

The little man paused and slowly turned around. "Who? Birdie?"

"Yes. Who else?"

"Now there's a fine joke," Augie barked. "Wait until Roscoe hears—"

"I don't think this is any sort of joke, Augie. You are speaking of my soon-to-be wife."

"You want to make some gel you barely know your future duchess?"

Kingsley flinched a bit. He wouldn't say he barely knew her.

And unfortunately Augie saw that as well. "Demmit, Kingsley! You didn't! Not Birdie! Oh, this is a fine fettle."

Whyever did he sound so horrified? It wasn't like he'd ruined the Princess Royal. "It doesn't matter—she's to be my wife," Kingsley reminded him.

"I should certainly hope so," Augie muttered, doffing his hat and giving the brim an absentminded tug before he put it back on, his jaw working back and forth. As if suddenly he was the one with the devil of a problem.

"You know who she is—"

"Oh, no—"

"Augie, if you know who she is, you must tell me."

His old friend shook his head. Furiously. "Must? 'Fraid I can't."

"Can't?"

This time, Augie nodded. "Won't. Promised the chit I wouldn't. And you know me, good to my word."

Good to his word, indeed! Why, of all the traits provided to Lord Augustus Charles Hustings (and therein lack of) did his most shining one have to be "good to his word"?

Kingsley gave him the sort of murderous glance that used to have new recruits certain they were about to soil their uniform. "Tell me who she is."

Augie, however, was made of sterner stuff. "No."

"You rotten bastard," Kingsley sputtered as he began to rise in his seat.

"*Tsk, tsk*, no reason to disparage my mother. Besides, 'tis my brother Teddy that we've always suspected wasn't all Hustings—what with that ginger hair and those woeful blue eyes. Come to think of it, he rather looks like—"

"Augie! We are talking about Birdie, not your brother Teddy."

"Don't see why we can't discuss both!" he huffed.

"Then let's do so. You tell me where I can find Birdie," Kingsley pressed.

Augie went to open his mouth, but then his lips snapped shut. He wagged a finger at his friend. *Nice try.*

Kingsley groaned, slamming back into his seat, sending the horses prancing nervously.

"Might I suggest—" Augie began.

"What?" Kingsley caught hold of the offer like a drowning man.

"—you go home."

"Go home? Can't do that," Kingsley protested. "Have you forgotten—they've got that gel all picked out and waiting for me. If I go home—" He shuddered, for he knew exactly what would happen. He'd be pushed, prodded, and badgered to marry her.

Proper lineage. Good dowry. Well educated.

And he knew what he would find. A horse-faced, sad-eyed debutante with four Seasons under her belt and some very thin excuses as to why she hadn't already been married off.

Perhaps he could introduce her to that poor old sap Birdie's father was forcing upon her.

Now there would be a match.

"Go home, Kingsley," Augie repeated.

He shook his head. Not until he'd found Birdie and had married her.

"Go home, or . . ." Augie scratched his chin as he came up with the real thrust of his threat. "Or I'll tell my mother you are in the mood to marry. Today. To the first chit you find. If only to spite your parents."

Kingsley felt as if the bottom had dropped out of his carriage. "You wouldn't!" he said in a great exhale.

Augie nodded. Damned well grinned at the idea.

For he knew as well as Kingsley that if his mother thought such a thing, most of London would hear of it before the hour was out.

And it was as if he could hear Kingsley's panic. "Was on my way to call on her right now." He nodded down the street to his parents' address and grinned. "Care to join me? Tell her yourself?"

There would be no place in London Kingsley could hide—Augie's mother would have every marriage-minded matron with a daughter dragging the city—and the river—in hopes of finding his carcass first.

He'd never find Birdie while being chased by a horde of would-be duchesses.

"Augie!" Kingsley tried his best to sound murderous. It didn't take much effort, because he felt like strangling the man.

"Go home, Kingsley," Augie told him, making his bow

and setting off down the street, in the direction of his mother's gossipy salon, with the audacity to whistle merrily and swing his cane as if there wasn't a care in the world.

As if Birdie wasn't lost. As if the entire world wasn't bereft that she couldn't be found.

"Augie, you are a cold and heartless bastard!" he called after him, unable to turn his carriage around in the tight traffic so as to follow him.

"I'll remind you of that at your wedding," Augie replied with a great laugh.

"Find her, Augie, find her for me," Kingsley shot back, but all Augie did was airily wave his hand over his shoulder.

And if he hadn't picked up the reins and started for what was destined to be a wretched confrontation with his parents he might have heard Augie's reply.

"*I'll find her. That is, if you don't find her first.*"

It was some hours later that the Marquess of Somersale, the heir to the dukedom of Marbury, strode into Landsdowne Abbey, his family's ancestral home.

The pile of stones that would one day be his.

A life that was decidedly a far cry from the battlefields of Spain and Flanders. Honestly, a tent had always suited him.

Yet, there was no "Major Kingsley" allowed here, only the name that was lawfully and rightfully his.

Somersale.

Well, it was only temporary, he told himself as the family's ancient butler showed him down the hall, as if he didn't know where the dining room was located.

"Are you certain you wouldn't prefer to change before going in, my lord?" the man asked for the third time.

Kingsley passed a mirror and glanced at his reflection, knowing full well his mother would probably have vapors over his appearance—dusty from the drive from Town, not to mention the shadow on his jaw, and that it was evident to anyone he hadn't slept much the night before.

"No, Rudges. I haven't the time. I must return to London immediately."

The butler made a noise—a disapproving one—that suggested whatever he was about, it was folly for certain.

Which wasn't too far from the truth. Falling in love with Birdie was certain folly, but his heart hammered at the very thought.

All the way down from London, Kingsley had been formulating a plan in his mind.

In between images of hanging Augie off Tower Bridge . . . by his heels . . . until he told Kingsley where Birdie could be found or his boots gave way.

Whichever came first.

Yes, he'd have preferred to have confronted his parents with his marriage to Birdie a *fait accompli*, but then again, this was his battle to fight and better to have it won before he went and gained her hand.

Rudges stopped before the large double doors to the dining room and glanced over his shoulder at the prodigal son's rumpled appearance. He heaved an aggrieved sigh, apparently resigning himself to being the bearer of bad news, and pushed open the doors. "Your Grace, Somersale has arrived."

There was a heavy scrape of a chair as it was pushed back. "About time," the Duke of Marbury declared. "Where the devil is my heir?"

Taking a deep breath, Kingsley strode into the room, his entire speech planned.

My apologies to Parkerton and his daughter, but I cannot be part of any match where my heart is not engaged. . .

"Your Grace," he said, bowing to his father and showing him the deference the old codger demanded—even from his son and heir. As he straightened, he began the speech he'd practiced. "Father, Mother, I—"

Yet he got no further.

For there was a loud gasp from a few seats down the table and then another hurried scrape of a chair.

"Kingsley?" came the strangled question.

"**H**ow could you?" Arabella railed at the man who was now towing her down a long, dark hallway, and doing her best to ignore the way her heart was hammering.

Kingsley. Her Kingsley. He'd come to find her.

Well, her, but not her.

Oh, bother, it was all a dreadful muddle.

Yet here he was, Kingsley. Her Kingsley.

No. No. No. She couldn't think of him that way. He wasn't Kingsley, but the heir to the Duke of Marbury.

Oh, the devil take him. The Marquess of Somersale was supposed to be . . . well, poxy. And dull. And not so . . . so Kingsley.

"You made a fool of me," she rushed to continue. "Why,

you lied to me!" Arabella dug in the heels of her slippers—not that it helped her slow him down.

Behind them came the hurried rush of boots.

"Now see here, Somersale!" the Duke of Parkerton was calling after them. "What the devil do you think you are doing with my daughter?"

At this, Kingsley came to a furious halt and she barreled into his back. He glanced down at her, a regal cock to his brow. "I lied?"

She had the decency to blush a bit—for certainly she hadn't been terribly honest in her identity. Yet she wasn't about to concede anything, not right now, not when she was furious with him. "You are no gentleman."

"Somersale!" the duke was now bellowing and had nearly caught up with them.

Arabella glanced over her shoulder to see her father and the Duke of Marbury coming down the hall—the pair of them looking ready to commit murder.

"Oh, hell," Kingsley muttered, and then, catching up the candlestick on a nearby highboy, he yanked open the door beside her, hauling her inside the dark room and slamming the door shut behind them.

He threw a latch, just as she managed to find her footing and spun around to face him.

"I'll say it again, you lied to me," she said, crossing her arms over her chest and ignoring the obvious.

How she'd lied to him.

Oh, not really lied, just not been as forthcoming as she might have been.

And he knew it as well.

"I lied to you? Really, Birdie." He shook his head, that teasing light dancing in his eyes.

"Yes, you lied," she insisted, feeling some of the outrage in her heart melting away under the teasing light of his gaze.

He wasn't going to melt her heart. Not in the least.

"And you left me," she said, the words coming out in a rush before she could stop them.

As well as a veil of tears. She turned and dashed them away with her sleeve.

If he was going to be the heir to a dukedom, then she was going to be Lady Arabella Tremont.

And Lady Arabella did not cry in public.

Meanwhile, the door to the room rattled hard, followed by the heavy thud of a fist as it pounded against the door.

"Somersale! You let my daughter out of there!" Parkerton demanded.

"Birdie?" Kingsley said quietly, taking her hand and pulling her away from the door.

The room was much larger than she had first thought, a long deep library that took up nearly one corner of the east wing of the house. He led her to the far side, where a long settee sat in a secluded alcove.

"You are no gentleman," she said, sniffing through a new spate of tears and sitting down on the spot he nodded toward. When he handed over his handkerchief, she took it and blew noisily into it. "Why, you broke into that house!"

There, let him explain that.

"It is hardly unlawful when you own the place."

"Your house?" she gasped. Suddenly so many things

made sense. How he knew where to go . . . which window to open.

He closed the distance between them. "Our house." And then he gathered her close and held her, one hand wound possessively around her waist, the other brushing the stray curls away from her face, his fingers brushing over her ear, sending a jolt of memories through her.

"Ours?" Arabella shivered despite her resolve to be furious with him, doing her best not to think of a lifetime of nights in that grand bed, in that room that now held so many passionate memories.

"Yes, Birdie," he whispered, kissing her brow. "Yours if you so desire."

She looked warily at him. "Whyever did you leave me?"

"I only went to get something for us to eat. When I returned, you were gone."

"You came back?"

"Of course I did. I had grand plans for our day. After all, it was my turn to choose three things for you to do."

"Me?" She stole a glance up at him.

"Yes, you," he said, sitting down beside her. "After I discovered you gone, I searched for you high and low all over London," he told her.

"You did?"

He nodded. "Of course. You took my heart when you left. I rather wanted it and you back."

She had lost her heart as well, and with his declaration, she now knew without a doubt, she'd gained it back.

Her heart and so much more.

"Birdie, I love you."

He what? She could only gape at him. "You do?"

He nodded.

From the door came more pounding and threats. Now even the Duke of Marbury was adding his own complaints of high-handed behavior and insinuations of madness.

Kingsley shook his head, as if he'd never heard such nonsense, then shifted so he all but blocked the door. "I have traveled all over the Continent, and never spent a day in such joy as our day yesterday. Our own London holiday. I want that for the rest of our lives."

"But . . . but . . ." She glanced over her shoulder, where even now, from behind the locked door, her father was threatening to call for seconds.

"No buts, Birdie. The truest joy in life, I've come to realize since I met you, is having someone to share the journey with. I don't want anyone else beside me, save you."

Was he saying what she thought he was? Proposing?

Yet before she answered, something he'd said before teased her. "What did you mean when you said you had three tasks for me?"

He brushed a stray strand of her hair away from her face and tucked it back behind her ear. "First, I wanted you to wear that outrageous gown of yours."

Her brow furrowed, for it was hardly what she expected. "Whatever for?"

"I thought it would be the perfect wedding dress—"

"A wedding dress?"

"Well, yes. Because the second thing I wanted you to do

was to accompany me to the archbishop's office to obtain a Special License. I rather thought his face would be quite amusing to see when asked to perform a marriage ceremony between the Duke of Marbury's heir and some unknown chit all rigged out like a Flemish—"

"Oh, Kingsley, you are a wicked devil!" she said, swatting his shoulder.

"It is my list—" he pointed out.

"And for your third request?" she asked.

"Oh, it began something like this," he said, catching hold of her and drawing her close.

Arabella went willingly, for it was exactly where she belonged. In his arms and with him kissing her.

And kiss her he did. His lips hungry and full of passion.

Her body came alive, and she saw her life unfolding before her, days of adventure and nights . . . oh, such perfect nights.

Yet another furious spate of pounding began, for it seemed the duchess had joined the fray and was now threatening to have the entire match called off.

"Whatever are we going to do?" she asked, glancing again at the door. There was still a very Tremont part of her that didn't like to agree with her father—and give in to the match he'd arranged. The one she'd been so vehemently opposed to.

"What are we going to do?" Kingsley's eyes twinkled with merriment. "This."

He hauled her up against him and began to kiss her, deeply, skillfully, leaving her shivering, and when she'd all but forgotten who might be right behind the door, she let out of a rather loud mew of pleasure.

"Oh, Kingsley!"

From outside the door came an indignant exclamation from the Duke of Parkerton. "Bloody hell!"

And the door came shattering open.

Three days later

"What has you smiling, Justina?" Peg asked as the two of them shared breakfast.

Mrs. Spenser looked up, her eyes brimming with tears. "Our dear Birdie has done what the pair of us failed to do."

"Whatever is that?" Peg asked.

"See for yourself," the lady declared, handing over the morning paper. "Right there, under Announcements."

And even Peg, crusty, worldly Peg, had to smile at the two lines printed there.

The Marquess of Somersale married suddenly to Lady Arabella Tremont.
  By Special License.

EPILOGUE

Venice, one year later

"Whatever are you laughing over?" the Marquess of Somersale asked his wife.

The marchioness held up the letter she was reading. "It is from Aunt Josephine."

"Why, there's only two lines on the entire page—what could be so humorous?"

"She's giving me marital advice," Arabella told him. She cleared her throat and read it in a voice much like her great-aunt's raspy tones. "'Make love to that scoundrel as often as possible. Love, Aunt Josephine.'"

"A fine woman, your dear aunt," Kingsley said, grinning at his wife.

"Indeed," she agreed. "What did the letter from your father say?"

They had arrived in Venice just the day before and the British ambassador had sent over a packet of correspondence that had been waiting for them—including lengthy missives from both their fathers.

Kingsley snorted and began to read aloud. " . . . I do hope you took my advice and did not traipse over the Alps like a ragtag pair of Gypsies."

Arabella sniffed. "Hardly. We followed Hannibal's route. Write him and tell him we got on rather well, even without the elephants."

For it had been an amazing journey. Hiking through the grand peaks—starry nights like she'd never seen. Magnificent sunrises over ragged mountains. Bright little alpine flowers tucked alongside the rocky paths.

Making love in the little wayside inns that they'd found.

Traipsing indeed! It had been perfect.

"He also instructs us to make sure and dine with the Marquess of Nettleham while we are in Rome. He insists we continue on there immediately."

"Rome?" Arabella shook her head. "Must we? We only just got here."

Outside, she could hear the water of the canal lapping against the house they had taken for the month. The fabled city was a jewel beckoning them to come explore.

"It is your day to choose, Birdie," he said, rising from the table and taking her hand.

Three boons—one day was Arabella's to choose, the next was his. And so it had been since the day they had wed.

"It is my day, isn't it?" She grinned as she recalled the three boons he'd requested the day before.

The last one having taken all night to accomplish.

She sighed and curled into his arms. "I don't want to go to Rome."

"And as a gentleman, I vow to follow your every wish," he said.

She looked up at him, this man she loved, her Kingsley, and told him exactly what she wanted.

And as a gentleman, he set to work immediately . . . by slowly removing her gown.

We hope you loved *Mad About the Major*!

Be sure to check out the series this short novel ties into,

Can't get enough Regency romance?

Lavinia Tempest has only ever desired one thing: a good
match to a titled man of fortune. But her plans all come to
naught when she causes a disastrous pile up on the dance
floor at Almack's.

Alaster Rowland, "Tuck" to his friends, carries some of
the blame for Lavinia's cow-handed entrance into Society,
and worse, he's wagered that he can make her and her sister,
Louisa, the most sought-after ladies in London . . .

Keep reading for a sneak peek at the next lively, witty
installment in Elizabeth Boyle's Rhymes With Love series,

The Knave of Hearts

Coming soon from Avon Romance

Alaster Rowland woke up Thursday afternoon with a dreadful hangover and the foreboding sense that disaster lurked just beyond his door.

In other words, it was a rather typical day for "Tuck" Rowland.

Even as he began to stir, his manservant came bustling into the room, tray in hand.

"What's the damage, Falshaw?" Tuck asked as he reached for the steaming cup of coffee. No fine pekoe for him. He started each day with a bracing concoction.

"Your uncle has sent round a note," the fellow told him.

"That bad, eh?"

"So it seems," Falshaw said with an uncharacteristic note of censure. A real valet wouldn't dare such a tone, but then again Tuck couldn't afford the talents of a proper valet. However, Falshaw had his own unique talents—like being able to discourage creditors and making ends meet when there were no ends to be had, so truly he was the best man for his employment. "And you made a wager."

Nothing new there, Tuck noted, as he pulled on his wrapper and strode over to the window.

"Regarding a pair of ladies," Falshaw continued.

Again, nothing new. He'd wagered on more than his fair share of opera dancers and flirts. Why there was this one time—

"Ladies," Falshaw repeated, and this time the censure was more telling.

Ladies?

Tuck turned a skeptical gaze toward his employee.

"Lady Charleton's goddaughters," the man supplied, as if prodding at Tuck's lack of memories from the night before.

"Oh, God, no," he muttered before taking another gulp of coffee. That rather explained the note from his uncle, Lord Charleton.

"Yes, indeed," Falshaw replied, sounding a bit too gleeful.

If Tuck didn't know better, he'd suspect that Falshaw rather liked seeing his employer periodically roasted by his only respectable relation.

"I'm in the suds, aren't I?" It wasn't so much a question as an utterance, but that didn't stop Falshaw from happily answering.

"Aye, my lord." Then Falshaw told him just how deep he'd wagered.

Lord Charleton's butler, Brobson, showed Tuck into the foyer. "Your uncle will see you in his library momentarily." Then the fellow strode off as if he had just admitted a plague victim into the household.

Yes, indeed. It was as bad as all that.

As he stood there, shuffling about a bit nervously, Tuck heard something. Coming to a standstill, he listened intently.

Crying. And then a huge sniffle. The sort that would leave a perfectly good handkerchief utterly useless.

Yes, as bad as all that—and perhaps more.

He glanced at the door. The one that led to the street and London beyond. Where perhaps he could start anew. Join a circus. Ship off to parts unknown. Drown himself in the Thames.

He shook his head at any of those options. He wasn't overly fond of travel and the discomforts and inconveniences of being away from one's own bed, and he was a perfectly good swimmer.

The crying now rose in pitch and fervor, and jangled on his nerves. Bother, it would jangle on any man's sensibilities.

Besides, it wrenched at his heart. He'd never admit this to anyone, not even if they were to forgive all his debts, but a woman's tears were his undoing.

Tuck strode over to the door and pushed it open.

He immediately wished he hadn't.

Admittedly he'd been a bit drunk the previous night, but certainly he'd have remembered *this*.

The puffy, red face. Yes, she'd been crying, but that wasn't the end of the matter. Her dress was entirely plain and provincial. Her hair stuck out a bit in a few places.

But to her credit, it appeared she was nearing the end, for certainly much more and she'd risk flooding the carpet. The girl took a deep breath and straightened, as if recalling the words of some long past governess. Then her gaze became more focused, as if she'd finally realized she was no longer alone. And her eyes took on a wild-eyed rage that prodded him to consider making a hasty retreat.

"You!" she gasped, stalking forward with all the fury of, well, a fury.

Alaster Rowland was many things. A fool wasn't one of

them. He took as many steps backward as he could until he bumped into the wall, having misjudged the angle of his retreat.

Now he was trapped.

Even with his back to the wall, he tried to reel back a bit. The woman hunting him was a veritable horror. A wet, hot mess of tears and scalding anger.

She couldn't be the same chit he'd met last night, the one who he had the vaguest recollection had been quite fetching.

"You wretched, horrible man!"

Apparently his memory wasn't as good as he'd hoped. But certainly he hadn't been *that* drunk.

"How could you?" she raged, wagging a finger at him. "You've ruined me!"

Ruined her?

He wanted to rush in and assure her, having taken a second glance at that lady, that he could promise her with all certitude that nothing of the sort had happened.

He'd have remembered taking this descendant of Medusa to his bed.

Meanwhile, the lady in question had dissolved into another spate of tears. Her snuffling and sniffing had him digging in his coat for his handkerchief, which he surrendered like a white flag.

She managed a gulping sob that seemed to quell her tears, and then she blew into the poor, hapless square of linen, trumpeting like an ailing swan, a sound that nearly split his ears and pierced the last remnants of his hangover.

Having continued to blow and snuffle—good heavens, how much more could there be inside such a petite thing?—

she finally finished with one last shuddering sob, and then offered his handkerchief back.

"Um, you can keep that," he offered. "Miss Tempest, isn't it?"

She had turned from him and was dabbing at the corners of her eyes—as if there was a dry spot left on that bit of cloth.

"Of course I am Miss Tempest," she snapped. "We met last night." Then slowly, and almost warily her head tipped toward him, her gaze sweeping up to meet his, her eyes finally widening as she came to a shocked realization. "You don't remember me."

He'd wager he wouldn't easily forget the fire blazing in her eyes at that moment. Clear blue eyes that left no doubt what the lady thought of him.

"I wouldn't say that precisely," he offered. "But certainly you were wearing a different gown—" Lord, he hoped she was wearing a different gown—for the one she had on was positively dreadful.

She snorted and took another step back from him. "Whyever did you let go of me? I was dancing."

Tout au contraire. He was neck-deep in a wager that proved beyond a doubt that what she'd been doing the previous night was anything but dancing.

"And now you've ruined me," she finished.

"I hardly think I've done all that," he told her, doing his best to glance in any direction but hers.

Yet he found it an impossible feat. Like when one happened upon a carriage accident and everything is a tangle.

How can one not look?

Nor would this chit be ignored. "You let go of me."

Glancing at her, he doubted anyone would blame him for abandoning her.

"And now," she began, until another bout of sniffles and gulps and some noise with which he was utterly unfamiliar came choking out of her, leaving him just a bit fearful.

"And now?" he prompted, if only to be done with all this.

"Everything is lost. If only I hadn't fallen into . . . fallen into . . ." At this she flopped down on the settee and continued to cry, leaving him aimlessly adrift in the middle of the room.

"Miss Tempest, I am—" he began.

"I know what you are. And now all is lost." Sniff. "We are both ruined. My sister and I." Sniff. Sniff. "We'll be sent home for certain. Today, if not tomorrow."

He hadn't truly been listening, for he'd been rather horrified to see the fate of his handkerchief, but a few words stuck in his ears.

Namely, "sent home" and "today, if not tomorrow."

Sent home? But if the Tempest sisters went home . . . However would he win his wager?

Winnings he needed desperately. No, no, no, this would never do. And so he told her.

"Home? I hardly see why. Besides, Uncle wouldn't be so cruel as to send you both—"

"He won't have a choice," she declared, waving what was once a proudly white bit of linen that now sagged in surrender. "Did you look at the salver when you came in?"

"Well, no—" Since it wasn't something he usually noticed.

"It is empty," she told him, with another shuddering sigh of despair. "Empty!"

His brow furrowed up.

"Mr. Rowland, if ever there was clearer evidence that my sister and I are ruined it is that empty salver out there. Your uncle will have no choice but to send us home."

Now it was Tuck's turn to sag down onto the settee beside her, for suddenly he couldn't breathe.

If he couldn't win this wager, he'd be forced to . . .

He didn't want to think of what he would be forced to do.

Decamp to God knows where. For this time Charleton would cut him off. Blame him for this mess, just as Miss Tempest was now.

He stole a glance over at the lady beside him, and listened as she went on about all the things that she'd never have now—a decent match, a good home, a marriage of some note—and knew that this was a tragedy of epic proportions.

His, to be exact. Everything she desired was suddenly everything he did as well.

"All is not lost, Miss Tempest. Never is," he began, Uncle Hero's words coming out of nowhere.

"I don't see how—"

"London society is terribly fickle—one day you are on the outs, and the next an Original, a Diamond to be desired by one and all."

"A Diamond?" she managed, her eyes brightening at the notion.

That was it. That tiny spark was enough to relight his memories of the night before.

Good heavens, she could be rather fetching—though right now it was nearly impossible to see past the red nose and blotchy complexion.

Her eyes, though puffy and red-rimmed as they were, still twinkled with a bit of hope and something else.

Determination.

And with that determined light in her eyes, he had to admit, she lent him a bit of hope as well.

He looked her over again, pulling from his memory the image of an elegant young lady. Breathtaking, really, if his unreliable recollections could be trusted. And if he was right, then yes, she had everything possible to make this happen. With a little help. And time.

Oh, demmit, time. That was a bit of a problem. How long did he have? A fortnight. Now it was his turn to shudder. A fortnight? What had he been thinking?

That was just it—he hadn't been.

"Miss Tempest, you must have faith," he told her, getting to his feet. There was much to be done.

"But—" she began.

He wasn't listening. "You must trust me—"

"Trust you?" Her astonishment all but filled the room.

Well, it wasn't like he'd asked her to dance half naked at the opera.

"Yes, you must trust me. Because I can put this all to rights. I can." He tried to sound far more confident than he felt.

After all, he had only two bloody weeks to pull off this miracle.

"You can?" There it was again, that bit of hope. But all too quickly she quashed it. "I don't see how—"

"Believe me, you will," he promised, holding out his hand to her. "Let me be your guide."

She stared at his hand, much as she had earlier given such scant regard to his handkerchief.

Oh, his poor handkerchief. He'd mourn the loss later.

"I cannot dance," she told him, taking his hand and letting him pull her to her feet.

"You were last night." At least he thought she'd been, before he'd . . . Well, no use in going over what happened. It had and it was done. Now it was time to move forward.

"Nothing but a fluke," she said, glancing down at the floor. Or perhaps her feet.

"Come now, Miss Tempest," he said softly, coaxing her to look up at him. "Will you allow me the privilege of helping you find your perfect match?"